Tara Menon is an Assistant Professor in the Department of English at Harvard University. Her writing has appeared in the *New York Times Book Review*, *Nation*, *Paris Review* and *Public Books*, where she co-edits the Literary Fiction section. Tara was born in India, grew up in Singapore, spent a decade in New York, and currently lives in Cambridge, Massachusetts.

Under Water

Tara Menon

Summit
Books

London · New York · Amsterdam/Antwerp · Sydney/Melbourne · Toronto · New Delhi

First published in Great Britain by Summit Books, an imprint of
Simon & Schuster UK Ltd, 2026

First published in the United States by Riverhead Books, an imprint of
Penguin Random House LLC, 2026

Copyright © Tara Menon, 2026

The right of Tara Menon to be identified as author of this work has been asserted in accordance
with the Copyright, Designs and Patents Act, 1988.

1 3 5 7 9 10 8 6 4 2

Simon & Schuster UK Ltd, 1st Floor, 222 Gray's Inn Road
London WC1X 8HB

For more than 100 years, Simon & Schuster has championed authors and the stories they create. By respecting the copyright of an author's intellectual property, you enable Simon & Schuster and the author to continue publishing exceptional books for years to come. We thank you for supporting the author's copyright by purchasing an authorised edition of this book.
No amount of this book may be reproduced or stored in any format, nor may it be uploaded to any website, database, language-learning model, or other repository, retrieval, or artificial intelligence system without express permission. All rights reserved. Enquiries may be directed to Simon & Schuster, 222 Gray's Inn Road, London WC1X 8HB or
RightsMailbox@simonandschuster.co.uk

Simon & Schuster Australia, Sydney
Simon & Schuster India, New Delhi

www.simonandschuster.co.uk
www.simonandschuster.com.au
www.simonandschuster.co.in

The authorised representative in the EEA is Simon & Schuster Netherlands BV, Herculesplein 96,
3584 AA Utrecht, Netherlands. info@simonandschuster.nl

Simon & Schuster strongly believes in freedom of expression and stands against
censorship in all its forms. For more information, visit BooksBelong.com.

A CIP catalogue record for this book is available from the British Library

'Metamorphoses' by Ovid translated by A.D. Melville (*Oxford University Press*, 2008),
Translation © A.D. Melville, 1986, is reproduced with permission of
Oxford University Press via PLS Clear

Book design by Alexis Sulaimani

Hardback ISBN: 978-1-3985-4915-9
Trade paperback ISBN: 978-1-3985-4916-6
eBook ISBN: 978-1-3985-4917-3
Audio ISBN: 978-1-3985-4918-0

*This book is a work of fiction. Names, characters, places and incidents are either a product
of the author's imagination or are used fictitiously. Any resemblance to actual people living or dead,
events or locales is entirely coincidental.*

Printed and Bound in the UK using 100% Renewable Electricity at CPI Group (UK) Ltd

For Shobha, my mother,
to whom I owe everything

Sunday

What novelty is worth that sweet
monotony where everything is known and
loved because it is known?

George Eliot

Upon species after species of island life,
the black night of extinction has fallen.

Rachel Carson

I measure every Grief I meet
With narrow, probing, Eyes—
I wonder if It weighs like mine—
Or has an Easier size.

Emily Dickinson

I am sitting in an upscale restaurant – crisp white tablecloths, polished silverware, uniformed waiters – at a table with three men. The room is loud with conversation and laughter. Four waiters approach in synchrony and lay down plates of whole fish in front of each of us. Hands pour more wine, and we start to eat, lifting chunks of white flesh off the bone with forks and knives.

Suddenly, the man directly across from me starts to choke. His face turns pink then red then purple. No one moves to help him because they too are holding their throats, gasping for air. He puts his hand over his mouth and coughs, a sudden violent movement. He lowers his hand and reveals a human finger, its nail painted glittery midnight blue. The man to my right coughs up a ball of long black hair. The man to my left reaches into his mouth and pulls out a little toe encircled by a silver ring with stars on it. The restaurant is alive with coughing, choking, spluttering, gasping, spitting, retching. A woman holds up an ear. Another woman, a nose. A thumb, flung across the room, lands on our table. The screaming grows louder and louder.

I feel a tickle in my throat and I try to suppress it. I know what is coming. I swallow hard, but my mouth has run dry. I reach for my glass of water to wash it down but when I open my mouth for a sip, I can't stop it. I cough.

Your eye rests in my palm, looking up at me, brown eyelashes curled and wet.

1.

NEW YORK, Sunday, 28 October 2012

The bright green leaves of the chilli plant on my windowsill catch the sunlight, and its tiny bloodred fingers reach toward the ceiling. A breeze comes through the open window, making the leaves cast dancing shadows on the wall. The morning light exposes the spidery cracks in the paint and I trace the largest one with the nail of my index finger. When my downstairs neighbour slams his front door, the neat square of sunshine on the wall shakes slightly then settles. I pluck the biggest chilli from the top of the plant, squeeze it hard between my finger and thumb until it splits and the tiny egg-white seeds burst out. I put the broken fruit into my mouth so I can suck on it slowly, and then I rub my lips and neck and chest with my stained fingertips. The chillis remind me of home.

When I wake from the nightmares, I start the day like this. As always, it doesn't take long. My mouth lights up with heat, my skin prickles then burns, my flesh on fire. My face grows hot, my temperature rises, and sweat builds on my forehead and temples and starts to trickle onto my cheeks. Soon, my bottom lip is tingling, a thousand tiny needles pricking the soft flesh until it feels hot and full. My nose begins to run and I start to breathe faster. I have to suck in air to cool my tongue.

Mayans have a word for what I am doing: *huuyub*, to draw breath with a puckered mouth after eating a chilli. I close my eyes and try to recruit my parasympathetic nervous system. Long controlled inhale, one, two, three; even longer controlled exhale, one, two, three, four. I focus on the smallest leaf on the plant and let everything else fall out of focus until I feel my heart rate slow.

I learned how to use my breath to control my heart rate as a young child swimming in the shallow waters around the island where I grew up. *Breathing is the most important part of swimming*, Anurak told me once. *You must know how to breathe before you can swim*. Anurak could swim, without breathing, for eight minutes. I could do three on a good day. Arielle did four once.

The chillis of the Americas (genus: *Capsicum*) and the peppers of Asia (genus: *Piper*) are unrelated. Chilli pepper is a misnomer bequeathed to us by Christopher Columbus. Above everything but gold, King Ferdinand and Queen Isabella wanted black pepper. When Columbus didn't find India, he didn't find the coveted spice, but he did find the spicy fruit native to the land he stumbled upon. He called them chilli peppers to soften the blow.

Arielle and I spent our childhood collecting facts like this from the men and women – botanists, geologists, marine biologists, lepidopterists, conservationists – who came to visit our island in the Andaman Sea. After dinner one night, a Swedish journalist told us about *huuyub*. A graduate student from Rhode Island, eager to compete, told us about Columbus and his adventures. *Thai food*, he said smugly, helping himself to another heaped serving of white rice, *wouldn't have chillis if it hadn't been for him*. He looked around as if he expected applause, or gratitude. Arielle rolled her eyes at me and I tried not to laugh.

I let my tongue hang out of my mouth to maximize the surface area for the cool air. When that doesn't work, I clamp down on it with my thumb and forefinger to see if the pressure will relieve the burning sensation. I don't know why I bother when I know none of it will make any difference. All the pain I'm feeling is a result of a neurological hiccup. The capsaicin in the chilli binds to the same receptors that the body uses to register heat. My brain thinks my mouth is literally hot, as if I have swallowed fire. I try telling my brain it is making a mistake, and for a few seconds I seem to have taken back control of my body, but then I have to curl my tongue again to suck in more air. The chilli plant warns us of a danger that doesn't exist and launches our bodies into unnecessary overdrive. All systems fire to protect us from the heat that is not there.

We learned about capsaicin from a Dutch palaeobotanist. He drew little pictures in the margins of a newspaper to explain how the receptors worked.

Arielle and I used to have chilli competitions. We would sit across from each other at a table and eat whole chillis, one at a time. The only rule: the first person to drink or eat anything else lost. We jumped up and down, stuck out our tongues, shouted, screamed, swore. I used to torture her by slowly pouring a glass of cold milk and then setting it down beside her. I usually won.

When I've had enough, I strip out of the oversize T-shirt I wore to bed and get in the shower. I twist on the cold tap and step into water so frigid it makes me gasp. I let the water flow straight into my mouth and swallow large gulps even though I know this will not help. Afterward, I lie naked and wet on the living room floor and press a tea towel full of ice to my bare chest. I slip a single cube away from the rest and use it to slowly numb my swollen lips.

I have only two visible scars from that day. The one on my left thigh is dark and round, a perfect small coin imprinted just below my hip bone, and it is easy to mistake it for a birthmark. But the scar on my stomach is nine inches long and a white so pure and bright it leaps off my brown skin – it looks like someone took a butcher's knife and tried to open me up along the curve of my rib cage. The sun falling through the window is cutting my stomach scar in half so that the bottom few inches are in shadow. I lift my hips off the floor so I can see all of it in the light.

I knew her body as if it were mine – the three tiny moles on her forearm, the peach-shaped birthmark on her left shoulder that she hated, the tattoo of a sea turtle on her right ankle that matched the one on my left – but she will never see this version of me.

Last weekend, I undressed in front of a man I had met a few hours earlier and he gasped. When he collected himself, he asked, *What happened?*

I fell over, I replied.

When we had sex, he was very careful not to touch my stomach, as if he worried he might accidentally split me open again with a stray hand.

Several men I've slept with have reacted like he did, with gasps, raised eyebrows, mute shock. Some, like him, ask me directly about it, but many don't. Some even pretend not to notice it, and then we both pretend I didn't notice their reaction. I used to ask to turn the lights off before I took off my clothes, to spare them the distress, but recently I've stopped asking. Let them see. They will never know about all the marks that have disappeared. In the days after, when I couldn't sleep at night, I counted every cut and scrape and bruise on my body. I got to one hundred and seventeen.

My back is starting to ache from lying on the hard wood. I flip over onto my stomach and use the last ice cube to draw small circles on the dusty floor. I hear the high-pitched ping of an email arriving on my phone, and then another, and another, and I get up to check it. As I expect, each email has a document attached and a single word in the subject line, three orders from my editor: *fact-check, proofread, fact-check*. There is no text in the body of any of the emails.

I work at a travel magazine for the super wealthy. It's called *Cortés*. (I know.) My official title is editorial assistant, which means that the most intellectually stimulating thing I do is write unattributed copy to accompany photographs in our Top Five series. *Top Five Wildlife Destinations in South America. Top Five Resort Hotels in Switzerland. Top Five Island Retreats to Decolonize Your Yoga Practice.* I don't get to choose the top five. Instead, every week, I receive an email containing five photographs accompanied by bullet points. My job is to transform these ungrammatical fragments into dreamy prose.

Your readers should be able to close their eyes and be there, my editor told me on my first day, as he showed me to my desk and handed me a blue coffee mug, a lime-green Post-it note, and a packet of materials from HR. The mug was imprinted with a map of the world showing seventeenth-century shipping routes. The note said: SIGHTS, SOUNDS, SMELLS, TASTES, FEELS. The welcome letter on the top of the packet warned, in three different ways, that romantic relationships between employees were strongly discouraged and must be reported immediately.

Conjuring florid sentences to lure London bankers and Manhattan lawyers away from their luxury homes to the greater comforts of luxury hotels comes easily to me. I grew up around those people. At my desk at work, I have filled the welcome mug with adjectives scribbled on scraps of paper: *isolated, secluded, pristine, untouched, gleaming, wild, cinematic, sparkling, glorious, rugged, unblemished, spotless, deserted, spell-*

binding, magical, crystalline, tranquil. For each photograph, I pluck out three at random and arrange them into clichés. I spend my days writing sentences like: *With pristine sand and spellbinding blue water, this cinematic beach is worth the hike.*

In my second week at work, I made the mistake of writing about some fishermen in Goa. A few minutes after I submitted the copy, I was summoned to my editor's office, where I was swiftly set straight. *We go on holiday to escape people*, he informed me.

I did not repeat my mistake, but in the past few months, I've started writing alternate copy about each destination that makes the weekly Top Five list. I scour the internet for photographs for these B-sides – a young boy working at a construction site in Sri Lanka (*Top Five Eco-Resorts in South Asia*), an old lady butchering chickens in the Philippines (*Top Five Wreck Diving Sites in the World*), a group of teenage sex workers dancing at a bar in Mexico (*Top Five Quick Getaways from New York City*): *In a bar crowded with American tourists downing tequila shots, girls in halter tops and heels move to the music as they wait to be selected.* I print these photographs on the colour printer, staple them to my typed-up paragraph, and hide them in my desk drawer. When I do this, I think: SIGHTS, SOUNDS, SMELLS, TASTES, FEELS. The calloused hands of working children, the sound of clinking of beer bottles and drunken laughter, the sweet saltiness of grilled marinated chicken, the thick stretches of plastic bottles floating in the ocean.

A fourth email arrives. The subject line reads: *Top Five Beaches in Africa*. I open it and see that there are five attachments and a single line of text in the body this time – *send back by end of day tomorrow*. I wrap myself in a towel and open the email on my laptop. There are five photographs of beaches, each labelled by name and country: Trou aux Biches, Mauritius; Diani Beach, Kenya; Ifaty, Madagascar; Bazaruto, Mozambique; Skeleton Coast, Namibia.

I am not going to the office tomorrow – I told my editor that I had a doctor's appointment uptown that would take all afternoon. He wasn't pleased but he gave me permission not to come in as long as I got all my work done on time.

I click the photo of Trou aux Biches so it fills the screen. The sand is a soft ivory, the aquamarine sky outdone by the turquoise water. Empty wooden deck chairs, shaded by huge hot-pink umbrellas, lie in front of a row of palm trees. There isn't a human or an animal in sight. From Wikipedia, I learn that the town began as a fishing village in the nineteenth century;

that the beach was named the World's Leading Beach Destination at the World Travel Awards last year; that it is the most famous beach in the country for sunset watching. This last assertion has not been verified; it has no citations.

I flip to a booking website to read reviews of the nearby hotels, which are either ecstatic or scathing: *Simply paradise. Appalling service! Incredible staff who all knew us by name. Mouldy rooms. Slice of heaven!!* I abandon a review about an English couple's unsatisfying honeymoon at a five-star golf resort and start reading an article about the island's flora and fauna.

Mauritius was once the only home of the dodo. When Dutch sailors first sighted the birds at the end of the sixteenth century, they showed no fear of humans. Their fearlessness made them easy targets; I can't imagine their flightlessness helped. Some sailors complained about the taste. Nevertheless, the last sightings of the dodo came less than one hundred years later.

I open the Notes application in my phone and start writing: *Located in the district of Pamplemousse, Trou aux Biches is the most spectacular beach in Mauritius. Come for the blissful afternoon swims, stay for the breathtaking sunsets.* I flick through photos of a temple online until I'm ready for my next sentence: *Take a break from the sheltered stretches of pristine ivory sand*

and turquoise water to visit the island's largest Hindu temple, built in 1888.

Soon, I'm on a roll; I don't even need my mug. Diani: *breathtaking, flawless, sparkling*. Bazaruto Island: *pristine, magical, gleaming*. Ifaty: *wild, tranquil, astonishing*. I write the paragraphs for the first four beaches in twenty minutes, but none of the usual adjectives capture the terrifying beauty of the Skeleton Coast. I open a new tab and read more. The stretch of Namibian coastline where the rough swell of the Benguela Current meets the desolate Namib desert was named by an Englishman documenting a famous shipwreck. The remains of whales, seals and more than a thousand ships are scattered across the sand. San people, indigenous hunter-gatherers of southern Africa, called this area the Land God Made in Anger; Portuguese soldiers called it the Gates of Hell. Today, the gates to the Skeleton Coast National Park are decorated with painted skulls and real whale bones. This is not a beach for the readers of *Cortés*.

Once I am dressed, I pick two small chillis from the plant and carefully wrap them in a piece of tissue paper. I put them in my coat pocket and leave for the day.

2.

THAILAND, Saturday, 25 December 2004

It is blisteringly hot. The clouds have retreated completely, the sun burns down without filter, the water is still and silent. The edges of my vision blur and the world closes in. I shut my eyes and press a can of soda to my cheeks, trying to bring the peripheries back into view, but my hot skin quickly sucks away the little cold that remains in the metal. I can no longer concentrate on my book. Arielle is untroubled by the heat (her Thai blood, she boasts often, knowing how much it irritates me) and she keeps reading.

I feel something crawling lightly up my leg and lift my head just in time to see a sand crab poised to launch itself off my hip. It jumps and then skitters through our splayed limbs and disappears into the sand. A black-capped kingfisher circles and dives, pulls up a foot above the water and rises into the sky again. Arielle sits up, brushes the sand off her stomach, and scratches at a sand fly bite until blood trickles onto the hawksbill tattoo above her right ankle.

"Don't," I say.

She rolls her eyes at me but stops anyway. She picks up the watermelon rind lying by her foot and sucks it. She had tucked a whole watermelon into her kayak; I brought the knife in mine. We broke the melon open as soon as we got here and finished the whole fruit within minutes. My rinds are stacked neatly by my feet; hers are scattered across the sand. When she finishes sucking every last drop of juice from this last rind, she throws it at my tower. Her aim, as always, is perfect. My tower tumbles onto the sand.

"Oops."

I pick up the closest rind and throw it at her head. She ducks, and it only grazes her ear.

"You're such an arsehole." We both laugh.

"It's going to rain."

It is the dry season now, the season the tourists invade the public beaches, but there are still quick, intense storms every few days.

"Not yet," I reply. "We have some time."

Anurak taught me how to read the earth for rain: the sun gets too hot, he explained, it smells sharp and sweet, the breeze stills then thickens into wind. The second time Arielle stayed with us on the island, we spent the morning drawing animals in the sand. I stopped when the air turned sweet and told her we should go inside because the rain was about to start. She ignored me and kept working on her elephant. Two minutes later, the first drops grazed our cheeks. She looked at me as if I were magic. When we were back inside and dry, we drew more animals on paper, sharing my set of coloured pencils, until the storm ended.

Arielle and I met when we were seven, during my first week at school in Phuket. We were watching two boys chase each other in the playground until one tripped and cut his knee open. He started to bawl. Arielle, as if expecting this, rolled her eyes with the practice of a teenager.

What's your name? she demanded.

Marissa, I said.

Is your mum coming?

I don't have one.

She frowned at me.

She died, I explained.

Arielle frowned harder and then, after a few seconds of silence, said, *You can share mine.* Her tone was definitive, as if now that she had said it, it was settled. I felt immediately comforted by her steady confidence. When her mother stepped out of the back seat of a shiny black car that afternoon, wearing a tidy skirt and high heels and with glossy black hair that fell below her shoulders, I thought, *Maybe I can.*

Mae, Arielle said, *this is Marissa. She doesn't have a mum so I said we can share you.* Without any hesitation, Arielle's mother said, *Of course you can, Marissa*, and wrapped me in a hug. When my father arrived in a tuk tuk a few minutes later, I ran to him and told him I had made a friend. Before he could finish introducing himself to Arielle's mother, Arielle interrupted. *Can Marissa come for a sleepover this weekend?* He knelt down to meet her at eye level. *Of course she can*, he said, *as long as you promise to look after her.* She nodded seriously. *I promise.* He stretched out his hand, she took it, and they shook hands solemnly, then broke out laughing together. As my father and her mother talked logistics, Arielle told me about the hotel where they lived. *There are three pools*, she said proudly, *and I need a key to get into my room.*

When we got to the hotel after school that Friday, a broad-shouldered Englishman was sitting in the lobby with his feet on the coffee table, talking loudly into his phone. He acknowledged Arielle with a brusque nod, and her body tightened as we walked past him. It wasn't until later, when she was showing me the second pool, that I dared to ask who he was. *My father*, she replied, turning her back to me, and I knew not to ask anything more. As we explored every corner of the hotel all weekend and I caught more glimpses of him, I started to understand her reticence.

Arielle's parents had met while her mother was at university in Bristol and her father was working as a bouncer in a nightclub. They married quickly so her mother's rich parents wouldn't have time to stop them. Dismayed as they were, Arielle's grandparents bought the young couple the hotel as a wedding present. Her father never bothered to learn Thai properly, so her mother did all the real work of running the place: she instructed the gardeners, negotiated with contractors, ordered supplies for the restaurant, chose the soft furnishings for the lobby, bought gym equipment. The only task her father did without fail – when he wasn't off on one of his golf trips – was check the housekeeping staff as they left. They would turn out their pockets and empty their handbags while looking at the ground until he nodded permission for them to leave. Few of the hotel guests ever realized that the stylish, soft-spoken woman who asked how their stay was going was married to the boorish man who lorded over the staff.

It didn't take long before Arielle and I developed a routine – one that we've now kept for almost a decade. During the term, we spend weekends on the island. Anurak picks us up from the jetty after school on Fridays and takes us back to the mainland late on Sunday mornings. During the week, we stay at the hotel. Arielle had begged my father until he allowed it. *One extra mouth is no trouble at all for a hotel kitchen*, her mother assured him.

The villa where Arielle and her parents live is on the outermost edge of the hotel property, as far from the lobby and the breakfast restaurant as possible. Our life at the hotel is luxury: air-conditioning, television, freshly laundered sheets every day, beds turned down every night. In the mornings, we're dropped off at school in one of the hotel's fleet of shiny black cars.

The guests at the hotel are boring: rich old couples from Europe (or rich old men and their new young wives) and wealthy Indian and Indonesian families with young children, usually with a maid in tow, sometimes one for each child. On Sunday afternoons, after we are deposited safely back on the mainland, we escape the hotel as much as we can. Most of the shopkeepers and restaurant managers on the public beach know us both by name.

When school is out, we spend every day that we can on the island. The water that surrounds the neighbouring islands is always busy with fishing vessels and boats for snorkelling tourists, but you need a special government permit to get to the protected reefs of our island. Only the research project's two boats and the marine police are allowed to access them. Even in the high season, there are no tourists here.

We have spent the whole morning today on the small beach on the north coast of the island, swimming and reading, reading and swimming. The forest that borders the beach is so thick that we can't walk here from the cottage, but we come in kayaks whenever we can. We share the rest of the island with the adults, but they let us have this tiny stretch of sand to ourselves.

The sun has stolen the seawater from our arms and legs and left fat crystals behind. Arielle licks them off her forearms and then puts a thick clump of her hair in her mouth and sucks out the salty water. A few steps away, the invisible tide unsettles the sand and the grains cloud the water below the surface. The sand crab appears and disappears again. The kingfisher shoots toward the water and this time vanishes into the dappled surface. Seconds later, it emerges victorious, white throat puffed and proud, a fish flapping in its beak.

Two years ago, Matthew told us that the Latin name for black-capped kingfishers is *Halcyon pileata*. *Pileata* for *capped*, *halcyon* for Alcyone, the Thessalian princess who turned into a bird when she saw the body of her dead husband. *The gods took pity*, Matthew continued, *and turned her husband into a kingfisher too.* Every year, Alcyone's father, the god of wind, ensured there was a week of calm so she could lay her eggs at sea. Halcyon days. The kingfisher settles on a rock a few feet away from us and starts to eat her catch.

"I'm hungry," Arielle declares, her eyes on the feasting bird.

I pass her the bag of crisps I grabbed on our way out of the cottage. She tears it open and eats them, three at a time. When they are all gone, she licks the salt off her fingers one by one.

I can tell there is something wrong – she is biting the flesh of her thumb – but also that she doesn't want to tell me, not yet. She is staring at the bird again, but she's looking through it. I feel my chest grow tight, squeezed by her secret keeping.

"Kingfishers?" she says, challenging me.

"Crown."

"Or realm."

We both love venery nouns. We learn new ones every week and test each other on the most obscure.

My turn. "Doves?"

"Piteousness. You asked me that last week. Zebras?"

"Zeal. Moles?"

"Labour. Nightingales?"

"Pudding. I love that one. Heron?"

"Siege. Porpoises?"

"Confusion?"

"Close."

"Riot?

"Almost."

"I give up."

"Turmoil."

We return, half-heartedly, to our books. It's the assigned reading for next term: *The Mill on the Floss*. We have just finished *Tess of the D'Urbervilles*. I loved it, Arielle didn't. She was annoyed that we were supposed to love Tess more because she was beautiful. I told her she was being unreasonable, and anyway Tess is only as beautiful as the rest. She told me I was being naive. We agreed that there should have been more scenes with the other dairymaids. I am just ahead of her in the Eliot and I watch to catch her reaction to the dead rabbits. She frowns, shakes her head, and then throws down the already water-streaked book.

3.

NEW YORK, Sunday, 28 October 2012

The branches of the towering American elm on Seventy-Seventh and Central Park West hang low and crooked across the pavement, some resting on the brick wall along the edge of the street. Burnished orange leaves cover the cobblestones that have been pushed upward by the roots making their way beneath.

When I close my eyes, I can see her nestled in the hollow of a tree, legs folded into herself, chin resting on her knees. I can hear frogs barking in the distance and a thick mess of the dark green leaves rubbing against one another in the wind.

My favourite trees at home were the dipterocarps, the old-world hardwoods that dominated the forests, with trunks that stretched so high that the tops were barely visible from the ground, leaves that stole all the sunlight, and roots that ran riot along the forest floor. Arielle preferred the plants of the understorey: wild gingers, orchids, rhododendrons. She would forage in the near darkness and take back what she thought was edible to my father. He would show her how to trim the plants, explaining which parts you could use for cooking and which you had to discard. I only understood how much Arielle hated her father when I saw how much she loved mine.

It took three flights for my father and me to reach Thailand: New York to Dubai, Dubai to Singapore, Singapore to Phuket. On the first plane, the stewardess asked if I wanted to say hello to the pilots. I turned to look at my father and he nodded back blankly, still stunned by grief. The stewardess looked like a perfectly crafted doll – hourglass figure, shiny black hair pulled into a slick bun, ruby-red lipstick to match her crimson skirt suit – and she smelled like green apples. She offered me her hand and I took it. My father followed in silence. When we reached the closed door of the cockpit, the stewardess knocked firmly three times.

The pilot opened the door and looked down at me. I stared up at him.

Well, hello there.

This is Marissa, the stewardess said.

Hello, Marissa, come on in.

The pilot and his copilot wore navy hats and crisp white shirts. The blue sky ahead of us was laced by clouds. The pilot reached into his pocket, pulled out a cherry lollipop and a tiny model of a plane – he explained that it was the same one he was flying – and handed them to me.

Want to see something? he asked me. He had a thick black beard and a lilting accent. I nodded. He flipped a switch above his head and put his hands on the controller in front of him. He tilted the plane to the left and the wing dipped toward the ground. My mouth fell open in surprise. Both pilots laughed.

Again, I said. It was the first word I had spoken since my mother died. I felt my father's hand squeeze my shoulder.

Again? the pilot asked.

Again.

He tilted the plane to the right. A thick carpet of fluffy clouds obscured the ocean below us. I felt a rush of delight.

Thank you, my father said to the pilots, *thank you.*

When I sat back in my seat, I used my model plane to mimic the movements, tilting it first to the left, then to the right. For years after this trip, I thrilled in turbulent air. I loved feeling my stomach flip after sudden drops in altitude. I loved the rolling of the plane as it was buffeted by heavy winds. Every time I heard the wheels unfurl from the belly of a plane with a loud click, I felt a wave of disappointment. Now, when I am in the air, I want absolute stillness. I can't tolerate anything else.

The entrance to the park at Seventy-Second Street is loud with the broken English of tourists and vendors: Spanish honeymooners trying to barter with a Senegalese man renting bikes; an elderly Japanese couple buying pretzels from a Bangladeshi man; an Indian family of five climbing into a velvet-lined horse carriage. The children look elated, the horse exhausted. Uniformed schoolgirls, a parade of hysterical giggles and tight white socks, stream out of the park closely followed by two women pushing buggies, talking to each other above the noise.

Stale pink carnations surround the IMAGINE circle; a single fresh red rose cuts the second *I* in half. I weave my way through the people taking photographs and narrowly avoid a collision with a cyclist hurtling down the footpath. The green grass shimmers in the sun and makes my head ache. Finally, I find my bench by the lake. I close my eyes and listen to the birds: jays, warblers, thrushes. I open my eyes to a tanager sitting on the sign that reads: WARNING ALGAE BLOOM.

A few minutes later, a man in a dark grey coat and red scarf sits down on my bench, puts his coffee between us, and lays the *Times* across his knees. There's an article on the front page about the nanny who murdered two children on the Upper West Side a few days ago. The mother came home to a bathtub full of blood. I read the first line of the piece over his shoulder: *She was unraveling.*

The man traces his wrinkled ring finger under each line of copy as he reads. He is a widower, this man. I can tell. Two women power walk past, dark patches of sweat on their T-shirts, pastel headbands keeping hair off their faces.

"Nothing will happen," one says. "It'll be like Irene."

"CNN said it's going to be bad."

"They said that last year."

They laugh in unison, and their scepticism makes my skin itch. The newspapers and news channels have been talking about a hurricane for days. No one is paying them any attention. I know I shouldn't but I want it to come in all its fury. I want to be where the Earth convulses again, where it brings people to their knees.

When people find out I was there that day, they ask if I lost any family. I don't know how to answer. Sometimes, I almost say yes. But then I get angry at them and at myself. I hate when people say we were like sisters. She was not my sister. You don't get to choose your sister. We chose each other.

When I say no, I see relief flood their eyes. I realized after a few years that there are people it is acceptable to mourn. The list of those you can endlessly grieve: a parent (if they die young), a spouse (if you are young), a sibling (if you both are young), a child (always). It is not acceptable to endlessly grieve someone who was just a friend. You must get over it after a period of time. People have told me that I shouldn't mourn her like this. Or else they ask, *Were you in love with her?* As if that could be the only explanation for this kind of grief.

There is no place in our language for grief about friends, or love for them. Our language is overwhelmed by the love and loss of lovers.

In college, I took a class on nineteenth-century poetry. We read the Romantics (the Big Six, no women), then the Victorians. When I read Tennyson's long poem about his dead friend Arthur Hallam, I felt like someone finally understood. *All of Tennyson's poetry,* the professor said in a lecture, *is in some way a response to Hallam's death.*

I read and reread *In Memoriam* every night. I switched the gender of the pronouns, slashing through the masculine with a black marker and writing in the feminine ones with a thin ink pen, trying my best to imitate the font of the book.

Forgive my grief for one removed,
Thy creature, whom I found so fair.
I trust ~~he~~ **she** lives in thee, and there
I find ~~him~~ **her** worthier to be loved.

In the lecture, a girl in the front row asked the professor if Tennyson and Hallam were lovers. She didn't think his grief made sense otherwise.

Poor girl, I thought. *You've never had a real friend.*

From 1953 to 1978, hurricanes in America were named after women. Since 1978 they've alternated: female, male, female, male, female. The hurricane two weeks ago was called Rafael; they've named this one Sandy. In 1988, the year we were born, two names were retired because they were storms to be remembered: Gilbert and Joan. During Hurricane Gilbert, a Cuban cargo ship was thrown into a shrimp boat in the Gulf of Mexico. Twenty-eight people died. According to the National Weather Service, the total death toll was 318: 202 in Mexico, 45 in Jamaica, 30 in Haiti, 12 each in Guatemala and Honduras, 5 each in the Dominican Republic and Venezuela, 3 in the United States (all in Texas), and 2 each in Costa Rica and Nicaragua.

Hurricane Joan, later renamed Tropical Storm Miriam, killed between 216 and 334 people in over a dozen countries in the Caribbean and Central America. When I read statistics like that, I don't understand them. Was it 216? Or 334? How do they not know? And how can they be so specific about what they don't know? Who are those 118 maybe dead people? In 2004, the total number was 226,408 or 227,898. At home, 4,812 people died; 4,499 are officially still missing.

Whenever the Earth revolts – earthquakes, floods, tornadoes, landslides, wildfires, hurricanes – I can't stop thinking about her. Since that day, I have become obsessed with disasters. In 2005, my first year back in America, a hurricane hit New Orleans and people stood on roofs waving desperately at news helicopters for help. One thousand eight hundred dead. In 2008, a cyclone hit Burma and Sri Lanka. One hundred and fifty thousand dead. In 2010, an earthquake registering 7.0 on the Richter scale hit just west of Port-au-Prince. There were fifty-two aftershocks. The chaos that unfolded in the aftermath made an official death toll impossible, but estimates range from one hundred thousand to three hundred thousand.

Each time, I keep the news on all day and strain my eyes as the cameras move over bodies, paying special attention to left shoulders and right ankles. Wrong time, wrong place, too late. But I had spent too long doing it to shake the instinct.

This week, I have been devouring the news for every advance warning about Sandy. I skip the weather channels and apps and go straight to the National Weather Service to look at the slowly moving patches of neon green and orange and red on low-resolution maps. I click through to short-range, medium-range and long-range forecasts. Every day, I watch and wait.

The American models all predicted that the storm would turn away from land and head out safely into the Atlantic. The Europeans sent over a correction: it's heading straight for you.

The man folds his paper and leaves. I stretch my legs across the bench and lie down. After a few minutes, a fly starts to hover, then lands on the sleeve of my coat. It has black-and-white stripes and rubs its front legs together gleefully, red eyes fixed ahead.

4.

THAILAND, Saturday, 25 December 2004

"Race you," Arielle declares, grabbing her snorkel and jumping to her feet. She sprints across the sand, bounds up the rocks that line the beach, then suddenly stops and laughs. She reaches down and in a single quick motion plucks a broken piece of shell from the sole of her foot. She wipes her bleeding heel on her other calf. She turns to face the water and throws the shell as far as she can. I watch the muscles in her back ripple and relax, then see her chin raise an inch, proud of the distance the shell travelled. She jumps and tucks herself into a ball before she hits the water.

I reach the top of the rocks in time to watch the sea snatch them both. I dive in after her, landing, as we both know how, in the gap in the reef. I revel in the water's embrace and open my eyes to a thick mess of glassfish, their tiny translucent bodies convulsing in unison as if obeying an invisible conductor. I kick myself forward and watch them slip away from me and find one another again.

The reef is busy with colour: fiery scorpion fish, yellow frogfish, red snappers, white-and-orange clown fish, a shoal of electric-blue angelfish, fat black sea cucumbers, powder-blue surgeonfish. A pair of Moorish idols gently probe the coral with their long snouts while a single dog-faced pufferfish with a Dalmatian coat floats past them. The white eyes of a moray eel stare as a shiver of reef sharks patrol the rocks. Sand suspended beneath the dimpled surface glitters in the sunlight.

When I come up for air, Arielle is still underwater. I fill my lungs and go back down. I find her cross-legged, hovering inches above the sand, and I am struck afresh by her beauty. In the ghostly blue cast of the shallow water, she is ethereal. Slowly moving rays of light caress her round cheeks, and the water holds her dark hair up above her shoulders. Arielle can walk into a room and stun it into wordlessness. I sometimes feel invisible beside her. I mostly don't mind.

Her thick eyebrows furrow as she stares at a spot on the sea floor about six feet away from me. She looks up and gestures me over with the quick three-fingered wave that we use with each other – *Come here, trust me* – and I go, as if pulled by a string. I swim through a pocket of cold water, kicking harder to warm up my legs. Together we watch a sea snake, black-and-white stripes, dart between the rocks in search of a luckless eel, until we run out of air and leave her to her hunt.

We surface together and float for a few minutes – me on my back, Arielle on her stomach with her face in the water. She grabs my hand hard under the water before she comes up for a breath.

"Riss, they're here!"

I almost don't believe her. The mantas hardly ever come to the west of the island. But when I flip onto my stomach to look below the surface, there they are, six of them gliding through the water, huge inky wings flapping, with a style and drama unmatched by the other sea creatures.

A squadron of mantas. Neither of us thinks that *squadron* suits; there is nothing militaristic about their movements. We have tried to come up with alternatives: a majesty of mantas, an elegance of mantas, a soaring of mantas, a magnificence of mantas.

We kick our way to the bottom. From below, we can see the black markings on their soft white undersides, Rorschach patterns by which we can identify each one. Anna K, Flo-Jo, Isabel, Serena, Lizzie and Lily. (Rosie gave us naming privileges a few years earlier. I named them after fictional characters; Arielle chose her favourite athletes.)

We've known these rays since we first started diving on the island. Anna K is shy but likes to stay close to the action. Flo-Jo is playful, sometimes even mischievous. Isabel is aloof, Serena bold. Lily, perhaps the most stunning of them all, isn't quite as intelligent as the others. I turn my body horizontal so I can float just above the reef. Lizzie, my favourite, approaches from above, blocking out the sun. She is huge – her wingspan measures just under seven metres. Blood trails from her right dorsal fin, and butterfly fish gather to clean the wound. Serena and Anna K form a patient line behind her, waiting their turn. All three of them are pregnant.

Arielle and I spend every day we can in the ocean, diving among the corals, or in the forest, losing ourselves in the trees. We know how to judge the waves, the way the tides shift later and later day by day until the pattern reverses. We know the movement of currents on every side of the island, how to swim out of a rip, how the colours of the water change depending on the sky. We know what the birds eat, how they mate, what they sound like, when they migrate. We know which plants flower and when, which are poisonous and which we can pick and eat. We know what time the zebra sharks hunt, which fish the moray eels eat, the names of the corals, the difference between blue-ringed and blueface angelfish, when the turtles leave the water to lay their eggs, which species feed in the shallow waters of the mangrove, which animals we can swim next to and which to give distance.

Most of all, we know everything there is to know about manta rays. We know how often they gather, first to feed and then to get cleaned by the legions of smaller fish who tend to them. Even though they are fish, mantas resemble large mammals: slow reproductive cycles, long lifespans, live offspring. We have never witnessed it, but mantas have to come together physically to mate. They gestate for twelve months and take at least a year off between pregnancies – they are among the ocean's least productive species. They have the largest brains of all fish, and distinct personalities. They are gentle, intelligent, often curious creatures who are capable of both socializing and suffering. Alien in their beauty, they never fail to hypnotize us.

Arielle swims to me and turns her body so it is perpendicular to mine, and our feet almost touch. She opens and closes her mouth slowly to release five perfect rings of air. On cue, Anna K swims toward us so that the rising bubbles will burst on her belly. She dips her right fin, as if saying thank you, then swims back to the others. Arielle follows. I want to go with her, but my chest has started to tighten and I have to surface for more air.

When we emerge from the water, two long-tailed macaques are play-fighting on the sand. They stop when we get closer and sit upright to stare at us with their big brown eyes. They get bored quickly, and one of them starts using a rock to break open an oyster as the other watches.

We head to the mangroves to seek shelter under a jackfruit tree. The leaves catch and split the sunlight. The sand is grittier here and it sticks between my toes. Arielle stays on the bank but I dive into the cool water. I plant my hands in the mud at the bottom of the stream and send my legs above the surface. In a second, Arielle's hands are on them. Before she can push me over, I tip myself backward. I pop my head out of the water, keeping most of my body below the surface to stay cool.

"What's wrong?" I finally ask.

"Do you think they're sleeping together?"

I know she is talking about Nik and Katerina, the two graduate students who have just arrived for the season, but I want her to say it.

"Who?"

She looks at me, daring me to ask again.

"I don't know," I say, even though I think I do. "Do you?"

"She's out of his league."

She's jealous, I think. *How absurd.*

"I don't know, he's pretty beautiful too." I say it to annoy her.

She shakes her head sulkily. She is always falling for one of the visitors, and I find her yearning tiresome. I change the subject.

"I haven't seen Anna K without Sita for ages."

"Yeah, and Kitty. She's always with them as well." Arielle is easy to distract.

The roots on the other side of the mangrove rustle; a heron is hunting in the shallow water, using her bright yellow feet as bait.

"Yes, I think they are," I say.

She sighs and digs both her hands into the muddy sand. A low growl of thunder sends the monkeys scattering into the forest and the hermit crabs back to their holes. The trees start swaying dramatically, the clouds gather, colour drains from the sky, the sea turns a dark mottled green.

"Let's go," I say, over the wind.

We run back to the kayaks parked on the empty beach and pull them into the water, leaving deep marks in the sand.

5.

NEW YORK, Sunday, 28 October 2012

A group of bird-watchers huddle under a larch tree in a state of excitement. An older woman clutching a notebook and a pair of binoculars is explaining breathlessly to a curious passerby that Quaker parrots are rarely, almost never, seen in Central Park, but a sighting was reported in the area earlier this morning. Instinctively I look up and scan the red and brown leaves for a spot of lime green.

Quaker parrots were originally found only in the forests of Argentina, Brazil, Bolivia, Paraguay and Uruguay. No one really knows how they made their way to New York. Some people are convinced that a crate of them – imported for people who wanted them as pets – broke open at JFK. Others dismiss this story as fanciful and subscribe instead to the theory that owners, drained by their pets' need for constant social interaction, released them into the wild. I've read everything about the species that I can find online, but I have never figured out who is right.

Whatever the story, the birds have made New York home. They have grown so comfortable in the city that they know to build their elaborate, multifamily nests on electrical structures to borrow warmth for the winter months. The nests have sometimes caused transformers to overheat, leaving thousands of people without power. Electric companies now hire special wildlife crews to remove the nests carefully, without harming their residents.

The leaves in the trees above us rustle, and the bird-watchers press their binoculars into their faces and hold their breath. More rustling, and then a female scarlet tanager flies out and away. A teenage boy who is part of the group lets out a loud sigh of disappointment. The older woman, shaking her head at the boy's reaction, takes out her notebook to dutifully record the sighting. A woman next to them is teaching her twin daughters how to focus their binoculars. One of them is listening carefully; the other is pouting and sitting on the ground.

When I was six my mother died in a car accident. She was walking across Columbus Avenue when a florist's delivery van hit her. She landed on the pavement outside a jewellery store, dead before the ambulance arrived. I used to imagine that after she was taken away, people in the street stopped to pick up the free flowers scattered over the road. It was peony season. The flower company sent three huge bouquets of white lilies and a casket spray of peonies to her funeral.

My parents met at a conference in the Philippines when they were both in graduate school. Arielle and I found their love letters, handwritten on lined sheets of paper, in a rusted tin cookie box under a bag of rice in the pantry. They were written during a summer they spent apart, my father working on whale sharks in Western Australia and my mother researching rays in the waters off Sri Lanka. In one letter, my mother described being surrounded by more than thirty rays. *I stayed still and they swam in circles around me,* she wrote. *I wanted to stay there forever.* I handed Arielle the letter when I was done, and watched as she read it. When she finished, she looked at me and said, *I'm sorry you never got to dive with her.* I nodded. *Me too.* She folded the letter carefully, put it back in the envelope, and said, *I wish I could have met her.*

My father kept an album full of photographs of my mother in his bedroom on the island. In most of them she is on dive sites around the world – Sipadan Island, Barracuda Point, Castle Rock, Jackson Reef, Magic Mountain – jumping into the ocean, clambering back onto a boat, or suspended underwater.

One photograph was different from the rest. She is on land, in a loose black dress instead of a wet suit, sitting at a table with a plate of pasta before her, a glass of white wine in her hand. Her eyes are looking straight into the camera, like a challenge. I showed it to Arielle, and she said, *She's just as beautiful as you are.*

When I came back to America, I found in my grandparents' apartment a picture of my parents on their wedding day. They are on the steps of Manhattan's City Hall, my mother in a simple lace dress that stops just above her knees, holding a small bouquet of pink and yellow flowers, and my father is in a dark grey suit. They are looking at each other, laughing, my mother's head tilting upward, my father's body at ease. Neither of them seems aware of the photographer. The smile on my father's face is one I've never seen. Now this is the only photograph I have of them together.

My real grief should be for my mother. This is what people think, even if they don't say it. It is the biographical detail that elicits the most sympathy. But I was young, too young to remember much about her. I didn't really know her enough to miss her properly. What I know, I know from my father. He told me that she could eat a whole cake in a single sitting after a long dive, that she loved the great Russian novels, that she had terrible taste in music, and that, like us, she always wanted to be in the water. For her, a day spent entirely on land was a day wasted. *She named you after what she loved best*, my father told me. Marissa, from the Latin *maris*, of the sea.

Both my parents grew up in New York. My father's mother worked in a hair salon a few blocks from their apartment in the North Bronx, and his father was a doorman on the Upper West Side; my mother's mother was an architect and her father was a lawyer. My father's father worked at a building on Seventy-Third and Central Park West; my mother's parents lived two blocks north, in the apartment I live in now. My grandfathers never met officially (my father's father died before my parents met) but it is likely that they nodded a polite hello to each other at least once.

Before my mother died, I lived with her parents when she and my father went away on research trips. I remember from those times the then strange feeling of the cold white marble steps leading from the living room to the dining room; the doorman Cole, dressed in a dark grey uniform with crimson trimmings, giving me a piece of hard candy when we came back from the park; the neighbours' black cat Eureka, who would slip into our apartment when my grandfather opened the door to get the newspaper; the smell of fresh crepes and lemon zest in the mornings. After my mother died, my grandmother looked pained just to see me. *There is too much of your mother in your face*, my grandfather told me once, by way of apology.

Two weeks after the funeral, my mother's adviser, Rosalind Watkins, wrote to my father and invited us to come stay with her. Rosie, as my parents called her, was one of the world's most renowned marine biologists. In the early nineties, she left her university job and moved to a tiny, uninhabited island in the Andaman Sea, forty-five minutes by speedboat from the western coast of Phuket. She had worked out of a small hotel at first, taking a speedboat to the island at dawn each day, diving in the morning, then coming back to the mainland to test samples and write up findings in the evening. After a year, she started living on the island full-time.

What convinced him was what she wrote about the feeding station just north of the island: *The mantas come every day, dozens of them.* My father read the letter and whisked me away. Almost immediately after we arrived, he set his own work aside and dedicated himself to the work my mother couldn't finish, joining Rosie in studying the reproductive lives of the manta rays: courtship, copulation, gestation and birth. With the help of my father, Rosie continued to publish in leading journals, entrusting Anurak to mail her carefully typed manuscripts from the post office in Phuket City.

Matthew had arrived a few months before us. A photojournalist from Goa, he had come to Thailand to work on a story about giant moray eels. After a week, he decided he wanted to stay. Rosie, Anurak, my father and Matthew divided tasks and created a life on the island. Rosie was in charge of correspondence with the outside world, orchestrating the constant flow of guests. My father ran the lab: cleaning equipment, running tests, checking results and supervising graduate students. Matthew organized food, did housework and made sure there was electricity and water. Anurak got the supplies and did all the odd jobs. Matthew and my father did the cooking; Rosie was incapable of making anything more than a fried egg.

My father had planned to stay on the island for only a short stint, three or four months to recover from the shock and the grief. It has been twenty years, and he is still there. Even now, he refuses to come back to the city he grew up in, the city his daughter lives in.

While everyone's eyes are trained on the tops of the trees, I look down at the ground. A small green caterpillar is battling his way through the mess of rotting leaves. The leader of the bird-watching group is explaining that they are expecting strange behaviour ahead of the storm. If anyone is interested, he continues, they are meeting right here tomorrow at 9 a.m.

There have been only two parrot species native to North America: the thick-billed parrot and the Carolina parakeet. The second to last Carolina parakeet in the world was called Lady Jane. The last Carolina parakeet – name unknown – died in 1918. One possible cause of extinction: deforestation. Another possible cause: women liked feathers in their hats.

I leave the bird-watchers behind and follow a twisting path through the Ramble. A few steps ahead of me, a couple is arguing softly, as if they don't want to disturb the trees. She wants to stay in the city; he wants to go to his parents' house tonight. "We'll be safer there," he says. She keeps shaking her head; he keeps sighing theatrically.

I force myself to stop eavesdropping on the unhappy couple and stride ahead to give them privacy. Suddenly I'm completely alone: the forest is mine. A ghostly white butterfly floats through the air and lands on a leaf by my shin. I kneel down slowly to take a closer look. It's not actually white, but a pale powder blue. *Celastrina neglecta*. It must be among the last of the season. Arielle kneels in front of me and places her hand by the leaf, palm down. The butterfly crawls onto the back of her hand. She stands slowly and the butterfly stays put, but when she stretches out her arm to bring it closer to me, it flies away and she too is gone.

The park ranger inspecting the smooth grey bark of an American beech is probably checking for epiphytes – plants that grow on trees but, unlike parasites, cause no direct harm. The relationship is commensal: one party benefits, the other is unaffected. Mosses and ferns are epiphytes, and so are most orchids. The ranger takes out a notebook and scribbles something.

In sixth grade, our class went on a trip to Khao Sok National Park to see *Rafflesia arnoldii,* a large red-and-white flower that blooms every couple of years and smells like a carcass. A few weeks before the trip, we received a letter from the school: *There will be leeches. Do NOT wear shorts.* Arielle's mother bought us loose, light trousers that were banded at the ankles just for the trip. When we got off the bus, the teachers warned us again to be careful about the leeches. *Don't show any skin. Cover your ankles. Tuck your pants into your socks. Keep checking your hands.* I heard a boy mutter, *Someone better get a leech.*

After many hours of hiking, I bent over when no one was looking and picked one off a dead leaf. It was black and skinny. I placed it carefully on the back of my hand, in the thin stretch of skin between my thumb and forefinger, and let it latch on to my skin. I felt nothing at first and then a slight pulling sensation. Once the leech had grown fat on my blood, I went to show Arielle. I thought she would be impressed, but she looked at me, half worried, half disgusted, and said, *Why would you do that?* I pulled the leech off, threw it to the ground, and didn't talk to her for the rest of the hike. The tiny hole in my hand bled and bled and bled. Arielle sat next to me on the bus. She didn't say anything but she held her thumb over the small wound the whole way back.

I emerge into the light and see a group of children chasing each other. They stop running to look at three turtles – statue still, necks craned toward the sky – basking in the sun on the rock closest to the bank. Two women, their feet intertwined, are reading on the grass, oblivious to the activity around them. A baby sleeps inside the V made by their legs. One of the women takes out a pen and starts scribbling notes in the margin of her book. I recognize it from the image of a woman weeping on the cover: *The Oresteia*. A few feet away, a black-and-white warbler lies face up in the grass, dead.

6.

THAILAND, Saturday, 25 December 2004

We are about two hundred metres from home when the storm breaks. Lightning fractures the sky, and seconds later the rain starts to fall in thick sheets. I hear Arielle laughing behind me and, even though I can't see her, I know she has turned her face upward to watch the dark clouds bleach white with lightning. She is the only person I know who loves thunderstorms more than I do.

All at once, I feel the water thicken underneath and see the beach grow farther away. The rains picks up force. I try to concentrate, pulling harder to make the same ground. I feel my arms and shoulders lose strength with every stroke. I see my father, Nik and Katerina on the beach. My father is waving us in.

"Come on, Riss, we're nearly there," Arielle shouts, as she passes me on my right and pulls ahead. She is showing off for the visitors but she is also helping me. With Arielle in front, I can match the rhythm of her strokes. She relieves me of the need to think: I fall into the strong, steady movement of her arms. Left, right, left, right, left, right.

My father, now waist-deep in the water, pulls us in, one with each hand. I expect him to chastise us for getting caught in the storm, to tell us that we should have come back earlier, that we should have known better, but he just tilts his head in the direction of the beach.

Squinting through the rain, I can just make out three dark mounds on the sand. Arielle runs toward them and stops suddenly, a few feet away. Her body goes rigid. I catch up to her and see what she sees: three mantas, dead, gills cut away, bellies up. Sita, Kitty, Elektra. The rain has washed them clean but they are circled by pink sand.

We step inside the cottage just as the lightning and thunder coincide: the storm is directly overhead. Matthew is cooking, and Rosie, in the corner facing away from us, is wiping down a speargun. She doesn't look around when we enter, and I know immediately that she is trying to calm herself down. Arielle and I are dripping onto the floor. Matthew leaves the pot on the stove to get us fresh towels. No one is talking.

Arielle looks at the speargun and then directly at me. I know from her face that she is going to reopen the row we had yesterday. She had wanted to stay on the island to go on the dives tomorrow; I wanted to go back to the mainland for a night out with our friends. We had bickered about it all day, Arielle insisting that going out was never worth it, me repeating that it was just one night. We finally reached a compromise: I'd said we could make it back to the island in time for the afternoon dive. But my father and Rosie are planning to tag the pregnant manta rays on the morning dive. The plan is to set up a way of tracking their movements to discover where exactly they go to deliver their young. The sight of the speargun, I can tell, has reminded Arielle of what we will be missing, and seeing the dead mantas has reignited her resolve to stay.

But before she can break the silence, my dad says, "Go shower." He speaks with uncharacteristic firmness and we both know not to argue.

When I come back out, Arielle is still in the bathroom. My father has taken Matthew's place at the stove. I go to see what he is cooking. I pick a prawn out of the pan and put it straight into my mouth. My father gently slaps my hand away. Rosie is still sitting on the floor, silent, and Matthew is talking to Nik and Katerina at the dining table. Matthew has an easy way with people; everyone relaxes in his company. Even the shiest of visitors unwind next to him, laughing as he regales them with stories, smoking his thin cigarettes.

Arielle and I were both here last Sunday morning when Nik and Katerina arrived: eyes heavy with jet lag, hair rearranged by salty wind, already slightly sunburned from the boat trip. The two men who came last season couldn't keep up with Rosie's gruelling schedule of four dives a day. After the third day, they asked if they could have the afternoons off. Nik and Katerina started working the day they arrived, and neither of them has missed a single dive. Rosie hasn't said anything, but I can tell that even she's impressed.

"There's been poaching before," Matthew is telling them, "but never in the high season. There are too many boats, and the tour guides and the fishermen all know each other. It would be hard not to get caught."

Arielle and I were thirteen the first time Rosie discovered the mantas were being poached. Three corpses showed up at a local fish market; a fisherman told Anurak, and he told Rosie. Their gills were missing, and the rest of the meat was being sold for next to nothing. Arielle cried when my father told us, then made him take us to the market the following week. We found one of the mantas lying dead on the chopping block:

Andromache. She was an inquisitive, majestic manta who loved the bubbles from scuba tanks. This made her a favourite with underwater photographers, because they could stay still, knowing that she would come to them. We had seen her on our very first open-water dive and had swum with her countless times since.

Arielle comes out of my room biting her cheek and avoiding eye contact. She's obviously freshly annoyed at me, but I'm guessing she's even more annoyed at herself for capitulating yesterday. She goes to sit next to Rosie, picks the other speargun off the floor, and starts slowly wiping it down. This is a performance for an audience of one. I get the message, but I'm not going to change my mind.

Arielle stops cleaning the gun and starts following an ant across the wooden floor with her index finger. She squashes it before it can slip between the floorboards. My father looks at me, tilting his chin in Arielle's direction – *What's wrong with her?* he asks with his eyes. He can always tell too; she doesn't make it hard. I shake my head and shrug slightly: *She'll be fine.*

"Lunch is ready," he announces.

At this, Rosie finally picks herself off the floor and Arielle gets up to help me set the table.

"I don't want to go," she says so quietly that only I can hear her.

"It's just one night," I say for the twentieth time.

"I want to stay," she says, raising her voice slightly, hoping that my father might hear and intervene.

"We'll be back by lunch." I refuse to relent this time; she always gets her way.

"Fine," she says, banging a plate down.

While the adults eat and speculate about possible culprits – a Chinese fishing vessel, a local boat supplying a bigger client, a single fisherman desperate for money – I take a gentler tack with Arielle.

"It'll be fun," I say softly, "I promise."

"Sure," she replies flatly.

"Come on." I'm still keeping my voice low enough that no one else can hear. "You always love it once we are out."

She looks straight at me and her face softens slightly. "Okay, okay."

Katerina can't talk about anything except the poaching. She wants to know everything. My father explains the relationship between the shark-fin bans and the increased demand for gill rakers. Matthew clears the table and comes back with a tray of steaming mugs of tea. He has put two tea bags in Rosie's mug. She takes hers strong, with a spoonful of condensed milk. Arielle doesn't drink tea, but Matthew hands her a biscuit.

Katerina turns to Rosie. "Can we do anything?"

"Not really," my father says, sipping his tea.

Rosie sighs, gets up and starts rummaging through the cupboards in the kitchen. Her rose-scented talcum powder is still visible on her neck. She comes back with a crumpled map that my father drew many years ago and spreads it across the table.

"We'll take the boat out this way this afternoon," she says, tracing her finger from where we are now, on the west coast of the island, along the southern tip, and then out farther, well beyond where we usually dive. "They are probably poaching from here," she explains to Katerina, pointing to a spot on the map.

"But we don't really know," my father says quietly.

"Or here," Rosie says, stirring her tea.

"Is it safe to go out?" Nik asks, pointing through the window. The rain has slowed but it hasn't stopped.

"Not right now," my father says, "but soon."

"We probably won't see anything," Rosie says, "but it's worth a try."

"I don't think we should be chasing poachers," my father says quietly. He is talking to Katerina, but really he is speaking for Rosie's benefit. The last time a manta was found dead, its gills missing, Rosie and my father had an argument. It was the first time I've ever seen them fight. He thinks they should just inform the authorities; Rosie wants to confront the poachers herself. Matthew refuses to take a side.

"We're not," Rosie says. "We're just going on a dive."

She stands up suddenly and her leg jolts the table. Two cups of tea tip sideways and soak the map. Matthew throws me a thick dish towel, kept on hand for this routine emergency. Rosie spills or breaks something at least every other day. I mop up the mess, and my father peels the soaking map off the table.

"Let's all take an hour to ourselves, and then meet back here," Rosie says. She wants to be alone. We leave her.

7.

NEW YORK, Sunday, 28 October 2012

From the edge of the fluorescent pond, I count forty-seven turtles swimming in the shallows. A bale of turtles. There are officially five turtle species that reside in Central Park, but I can see only red-eared sliders. In my last five visits to the park, I haven't seen a single other kind. The first sliders here were definitely pets, released by owners weary of the responsibility. You wouldn't know from watching these serene creatures how much damage they have caused. Along with the tiger mosquito, the house mouse and the common starling, red-eared sliders rank among the most destructive invasive species in the world. Sliders crowd other species out – they eat all the food, steal all the best sunbathing spots, lay claim to the nesting areas. And they are vectors of deadly diseases. Other animals perish in their presence. Between 1989 and 1997, 52 million of these turtles were exported as pets from the United States to foreign markets.

A little boy in a striped blue shirt is sucking his thumb and watching the placid turtles while his father ties his shoelace. The largest of the turtles moves his neck slightly and the boy's eyes widen. When the turtle pushes himself off the ledge and hits the water with a quiet splash, the boy's mouth falls open in surprise. He hadn't realized that the turtles were real. The turtle surfaces for a breath then floats serenely sideways.

I look out across the water and imagine that the large shadows are mantas gliding below the surface. Unlike most marine animals, manta rays can't float. They are negatively buoyant: they would sink if they stopped swimming. And if they stopped swimming, they would asphyxiate, because they would stop pumping water through their gills. Manta rays are destined for lives of perpetual motion.

Two turtles knock shells and then swim away together, their front flippers clawing furiously until they disappear into deeper water. My calf twitches. I want to swim after them. I dig my right thumb into the flesh of my left palm until the urge passes.

When we were twelve, my father took me and Arielle to a nearby island to watch turtles hatching. We walked up the beach until we could see the nest of eggs in the sand, then we stopped and listened. With the sound of paper crinkling, the baby turtles poked their noses through the shells. We put our goggles on and watched them flap their way out to sea. When we were thirteen, we found a dead turtle, choked on a plastic bag, next to a stall where a man rented snorkelling equipment. Arielle didn't want to touch the corpse, but she insisted that we bury it. I picked it up with my bare hands and carried it to a quiet corner of the beach where she dug it a grave, small but deep.

We were sixteen when I convinced her to get the matching tattoos of hawksbills on our ankles. My left, her right. She managed to hide hers from her father for a month by wearing shoes and high socks when he was around. One afternoon, when we thought he was still away on one of his many golf trips, we came from the beach barefoot and his gaze landed on her ankle before we could walk away. *What. Is. That*, he said. It wasn't a question, so she didn't reply. He walked away from us, grinding his teeth.

At dinner that evening, he asked Arielle's mother if she knew about the tattoo. She hesitated. *Answer me*, he said, hitting the table with an open palm. *Yes*, she said, looking down at her plate. *If you let her do what she wants*, he said, *she'll have no respect for you*. When she did not answer, he pushed his chair away from the table and left the room. Arielle looked at her mother, her eyes full. *I'm sorry*, she said. Her mother leaned across the table and took Arielle's hands in hers. *Don't say sorry.*

By the edge of the pond, a girl in a peach quinceañera dress is posing. Her father is trying to take a photo with Belvedere Castle framed in the background. Her mother keeps running into the frame to adjust the girl's tiara. The father keeps admonishing the mother to get out of the frame and telling the daughter to shift slightly to the right. The girl's smile is becoming so strained she looks slightly unhinged.

  A young man, lying belly down on the grass, is taking photos of the sunbathing turtles with a telephoto lens. Matthew used to tell me that if you wanted to be good photographer you had to get dirty, be patient, and react quickly. The man sits up suddenly to examine the photo he has just taken in the viewfinder, then flips back onto his stomach to try again, but by the time he is in position the turtles have slipped back into the water.

My father learned to love animals from his father. The two of them would come to Central Park every Saturday morning, the only day my grandfather had off work, to sit by Turtle Pond. The long rides were mostly silent, the two of them sitting side by side in a mostly empty car on the 2 train, but in the park, my grandfather would talk about his childhood in Trinidad, the trees and the beaches and the animals.

In the house where he grew up, turtle meat was frequently on the menu. He never really associated the gigantic animals he saw on the beach with the food he ate in the evenings until one night when he and his friends were playing football. As they played, the sun set and the light faded, but they could still see the ball by the light of the moon. A player on the other team tried to shoot the ball toward the makeshift goal but it flew into the sea. My grandfather went in after it. As he emerged from the water, his shorts dark and soaked, he noticed a movement a few feet away.

A turtle was heaving herself out of the water, her flippers digging into the sand. She was huge, ready to burst with eggs. She moved slowly but with steady purpose, pushing her way up the sloping sand and navigating the human detritus until she found a place to dig her nest. Turning to face the sea, she positioned herself over the freshly dug hole. The pearly eggs fell out quickly, one after the other after the other, until there was a large gleaming pile. With her hind flippers, she covered them with sand and then, exhausted, made her way back to the ocean. My grandfather didn't notice the men lying in wait until they stood up. They got her before she touched the water. He never ate turtle again.

In the southwest corner of Sheep Meadow, a group of men are playing five-a-side football. One of them miskicks the ball and it rolls near me. I chip it back and it lands at his feet. Despite the cold, they are playing shirts and skins. There is no rhythm to the game. One team barely completes two passes before the other intercepts the ball or it is sent flying off the grass. Next to them, four girls stand in a square, passing a rugby ball, right to left, then left to right. One of the skins sends a shirt to the ground with a rough tackle, and a brawl ensues. Only one person, a shirt, doesn't get involved. When I get closer, I realize it's a girl. She walks slowly over to retrieve the ball, forgotten in the scrum, and starts passing it against a large, flat rock, waiting for the fight to end. *We would be friends*, I think, and walk closer to watch her. She kicks the ball high into the air and stops it dead as it comes down.

I was decent at football, but Arielle was spectacular. She danced around players on the field, turning them inside and out. She left the impression of being everywhere at once. She was the engine of the attack, urging the team forward, leading the charge with sly runs down the right wing and deft crosses into the box. She was disruptive defensively – she could interrupt flow in the midfield, get back in time when the other team was on the counterattack to execute a swift decisive tackle. It seemed as if she could will the ball with her mind rather than her feet. On the field, Arielle sometimes looked like she was moving on air.

But playing with girls bored her, even if she never said so out loud. With us, she played with a restraint, almost a politeness: she felt she couldn't fight, shouldn't trash-talk, needed to be a good sport. The effort of it stifled her. For all her talent, she sometimes became passive and stuck when we competed against other schools. When she played with boys, it was as if she were set free. With them, she sought to dictate, to dominate, to humiliate.

The boys' coach saw her playing one lunchtime and got an allowance for her to play on his team. The boys resisted at first, and then relented after a single practice. They wanted to win. For her first game, she hammed it up. Before the warm-up, she folded her long hair on top of her head and put on a baseball cap. With her hair tucked away and her slender figure, she looked like a boy. Halfway through the game, when she had run down the field and put three of the opposition on the ground – a magic first touch, a nutmeg, a shift of bodyweight – she whipped off her hat and let her long hair tumble out. She waited for the gasp of the crowd (*It's a girl!*) and then drove the ball into the back of the net. Even onlookers who didn't know anything about football were captivated. *Men amongst boys*, I heard one of the fathers muttering – never mind that she was neither.

The men in Sheep Meadow have stopped fighting and the game resumes, but there is a different energy now, angrier, almost vicious. After two minutes, the girl removes herself from the game and sits down to change her shoes. None of the men notice. She takes off her playing shirt, slips on a long-sleeved black turtleneck dress over her sports bra and wriggles out of her shorts. She is a different person: stylish, delicate, an adult. She puts a pair of sunglasses on and heads south in the direction of the carousel.

A few minutes after she leaves, a small flock of grazing pigeons suddenly scatters into the air. One of the rugby girls shouts and waves her friends over. Everyone nearby stops what they are doing to stare. A few people get up and walk over slowly. Even the football game is put on pause. A semicircle forms around something on the ground. I walk closer to find out what has captured their attention: a red-tailed hawk. It has caught one of the pigeons and is dismembering it slowly, plucking out feathers one at a time, ripping out flesh. The hawk stops and lifts his head to look out at the spectators. Blood drips from his beak.

8.

THAILAND, Saturday, 25 December 2004

Outside, the sun is reclaiming control of the sky. The storm has passed as quickly as it came. When we reach the mangrove stream that separates the cottage and the lab from the guesthouse, Nik bends down to unlace his shoes but Katerina steps straight in, sandals still on. The stream is swollen from the rain, and the water reaches her knees. She closes her eyes and inhales deeply. She has a small tattoo of an elephant on her calf, its tiny trunk raised in salute. Her hair is the colour of fire and her lily-white skin is paler than the sand. Neither of us can take our eyes off her.

The catlike mewling of a Brahminy kite cuts through the air. Arielle looks at me. *Yes*, I think back silently, *let's go as soon as we are done*. The new arrivals are having trouble with the shower and we have come to teach them the trick. Arielle follows Katerina through the stream and I skip across the three large rocks that Anurak has laid down for high tide.

There are three small wooden buildings on the island – the cottage where we live and sleep, the lab where my father and Rosie run basic tests, and the guesthouse, which has four small rooms for the constant stream of men and women who come to visit for a few days or weeks. In addition to Katerina and Nik, there are two other researchers staying this month: Frank, an ornithologist from Germany studying the migratory patterns of raptors, and Sophie, an ethnobotanist from South Africa here to investigate the medicinal properties of certain endemic plants. Frank and Sophie have been here for three weeks, and they have spent each day, from dawn to dusk, in the forest.

Rosie has one rule about visitors: no one can spend more than a month at a stretch in the guesthouse. They are free to return, to come back up to three times a year, but they can't set up shop. Officially, this is to allow more researchers the opportunity to spend time on the island, to have access to the dive sites, the mangroves, the coral reefs, the rainforest. But really it is to protect the balance, to keep this place feeling like it belongs to the four of us who live here: Rosie, Matthew, my father and me.

As soon as we enter the guesthouse, Katerina pushes open all the windows and turns the fan on high. The doors to Katerina's and Nik's rooms are open: one bed is perfectly made, the other a mess of sheets. Arielle pretends not to see me watching for her reaction. She steps into the bathroom and shows Katerina exactly how to manipulate the shower to get hot but not scalding water.

"You have to pull the tap all the way to the right and then back a little bit," she says, "like this."

Katerina thanks her, and we head straight into the forest.

The leaves are still heavy from the rain. Water drips off the trees and falls in small streams onto the soft ground. A light breeze cradles the wet branches. Mud gives way under our feet. Black butterflies emerge from the shadows. We leave deep, uneven tracks with each step and I have to focus to keep from slipping. The light is starting to caress the plants of the understorey again. Arielle pulls back a large leaf to show me an orchid growing out of the tree trunk, and when she lets the leaf go, drops of water bounce into the air.

A few years ago, Matthew and a Welsh arborist built a tree house, tucked away in the depths of the forest. The first twenty minutes of the walk are easy, a wide and gently sloping path, but the final twenty, uphill, through thick foliage on a narrow path, take effort and concentration. Sometimes, researchers get lost on the way, even though Matthew has carefully marked the way by painting thin blue blazes on the tree trunks.

When we have the option, Arielle and I usually choose to dive instead of staying on land, but for the past couple of weeks we've gone into the forest every day. The first two days, we went with Sophie and she showed us how to collect samples. The next three days, Frank taught us how to record birdsong and how to identify the different species of sunbirds. Last week, we spent the afternoons by ourselves in the tree house, watching a pair of kites guard their nest. The chicks hatched three days ago – *I've been eating my lunch with them*, Frank told us over breakfast – but we haven't been to see them yet.

At the foot of the hill, before the real incline begins, we stop to peek into the red and yellow cups of a carnivorous pitcher plant: *Nepenthes suratensis*. Three black insects are immortalized in the sticky liquid. Sophie told us over breakfast last week that the Greek word *nepenthe* literally means without (*ne*) grief (*penthos*), but that it is better translated as sorrow banishing. My father overheard her and told us all the story of Pentheus, the man of sorrows, who was torn limb from limb by his mother and aunts. In *The Odyssey*, he added, Helen is gifted nepenthe, a magic potion that dispels all sorrow with forgetfulness.

"If nepenthe existed," Arielle asks, stroking the bottom of one of the red cups, "would you take it?"

"No," I say, without hesitating. "Would you?"

She doesn't answer. We are halfway up the hill before she speaks again. "Do you think your father would?"

"I don't know." I look at her, but she is looking straight past me.

"I think my mother would."

I want to hug her, but I know it would make her cry. We talk about everything except her father.

The cool brought by the rain withdraws slowly, then suddenly. By the time we reach the tree house, Arielle's face is glistening with sweat. I wait till she has reached the top of the ladder before I follow. I find her fixated on the nest, where the soft grey down of the heads of two chicks is just visible. The same pair of kites has been using this nest for the past three years. We've watched each year as they take turns bringing more twigs and branches, and the nest grows bigger and untidier. It's now almost doubled in size.

After a few minutes, the male returns with a dead crab between his beak. Two more fluffy heads appear. We watch as he feeds his young, then he leaves again, in search of more food. The female, perched on a branch a few feet away, stands guard.

9.

NEW YORK, Sunday, 28 October 2012

I loop back down to the southwest corner of the park and exit at Columbus Circle. Three men sitting in a row behind the wheel of a truck wave to me. I blow them a kiss and they nearly drive into the car in front of them. They look abashed. An older lady sees the whole thing and laughs loudly.

When I get to the entrance of the subway station, a pregnant woman is struggling with a stroller. I lift the front wheels and make faces at the little girl in it as I step backward down the stairs. On the platform, a lady is selling mangoes sprinkled with lime, chilli and salt, and I miss home so much I can't stand it. My throat constricts, water pools under my tongue, my eyes fill until they can't hold the tears anymore. I join the ranks of crying women on subway platforms. The vendor insistently holds out a packet of fruit. I reach into my pocket to check for dollar bills but she waves me off. "No, no. Para ti." She presses the packet into my hands and urges me through the doors of the just-arrived train.

In the subway car, a woman in faded pink scrubs is swaying her hips. Reggae leaks out of her headphones. A suited bald man who smells slightly sour scowls down at his phone. A woman is reading quietly to her daughter from a picture book spread across her lap: *"Please give me one of your shiny scales. They are so beautiful and you have so many."* The girl is resting her head against her mother's arm and sucking her thumb. Her hair is neatly braided into two plaits.

In my first month of school in Thailand, I caught sight of my tangled mess of hair in the mirror one day and burst into tears. Arielle found me sobbing by the sinks. *What's wrong?* she asked. I pointed at my hair and started crying harder. *I can fix it*, she said confidently. She came back a few minutes later with a tiny wooden hairbrush. Patiently, she started combing out the knots in my hair and talked without stopping until she was finished.

The man sitting next to me is chuckling over a free morning paper. I read over his shoulder: *Q: Why are hurricanes named after women? A: Because when they arrive, they're wet and wild, but when they go, they take your house and car.* A French ornithologist who had come to the island to study the vocalizations of blue-banded kingfishers once, after a few beers, interrupted the dinner conversation to ask, *Do you know the female praying mantis devours the male within minutes after mating?* Silence fell over the table as we all wondered where this was going, until he continued: *The human female prefers to stretch it out over a lifetime.* He paused, waiting for us to get it, then burst into laughter. *Oh my god. You're so funny*, Arielle said, donning an affectless Valley Girl accent. Even my father had to stifle a laugh.

I get off the train at Christopher Street and walk west toward the Hudson. At the river, a small crowd of people is standing still and looking up – against the dusky sky, a murmuration of starlings lifts and plummets, cleaves and converges. Children are pointing, even the eyes of adults are wide with wonder. A lone starling, determined not to be overlooked, imitates a car alarm. His glossy black feathers glisten under the fluorescent light of a nearby food cart.

On a patch of grass, a toddler giggles at another bird on the ground. "Seagull," her exhausted mother explains. "Sea. Gull." The child tries to clap as she steps toward the bird, but this is too much at once, and she falls over and begins to wail as the gull looks on, unmoved. Another woman is fishing off the pier while her son stands next to her, his hand gripping the handle of a plastic bucket.

When my father and I first got to the island, Anurak was

still a fisherman; he sold his daily catch to restaurants and hotels on Patong Beach and did small errands for Rosie to make extra money in the evenings. Each year, it became harder and harder to make a reliable living through fishing. After a week when he didn't make enough to buy food for his family, he finally accepted Rosie's offer to work for her full-time.

I press my body against the cool railing and let my toes hang off the edge as I look out across the dark river. A head is bobbing in the water. I nearly call out, but then I realize it is just an abandoned hard hat floating downstream.

For weeks afterward, the ocean continued to surrender the dead, presenting the broken bodies like offerings.

Unlike some people who were there that day, even fishermen, I am not scared of the water. Men who had spent every day of their life on the open water were suddenly unable to get into the ocean again. I got back in two weeks later, on the beach that used to be ours. But I am scared of the sound of distant engines, any low steady rumbling. I recognize people like me on the street. The woman who jumps when a ladder crashes to the ground, the girl who freezes when car tyres screech, the old man who gasps when a child shouts boo.

The little boy holding the bait bucket is looking up to watch a plane that is starting its descent. The left wing dips toward the ground, and I imagine the passengers peering through the thick glass of the windows to watch as the clouds give way to the city. I used to love landing in New York and looking down at dark trees lining invisible streets, the green of the foliage flecked by the red bricks of homes, skyscrapers bursting up from the concrete, slow-motion traffic dotted with yellow cabs, the grey-green Hudson streaked with the foam left by morning sailboats, the smooth edges of the land cradled by dark water. The pilot tilts the plane to circle around the southern tip of the island. The woman starts packing up her fishing rod; they have caught nothing.

I leave the river and head east. Arielle is walking next to me now, mostly staying in step, once in a while skipping ahead. Sometimes I enjoy the company. Sometimes it is too much. A teenage girl wearing oversize gold headphones eyes me suspiciously; she knows the body language of a woman walking alone, and my relaxed shoulders give me away. She looks behind me to see who I am with, and I see her frown when she finds no one.

Since Arielle left me, I feel submerged. I can't find my way to the surface. I never went to grief counselling. But after I found Tennyson, I went searching for the rest of the literature of grief. I followed Tennyson with Thomas Hardy, Hardy with CS Lewis, Lewis with Joan Didion. I read *Antigone* in a single sitting one afternoon in the stacks in the library. I kept

Auden in my pocket. I tried on all the metaphors. Grief is a secret. Grief is heavy. Grief is invisible but it is everywhere. Grief knocks the wind out of you. Some of it felt all wrong, like they had no idea, and some of it felt as if I had written the words myself.

In his book about losing his wife, Lewis writes, *No one ever told me that grief felt so like fear. I am not afraid, but the sensation is like being afraid. The same fluttering in the stomach, the same restlessness, the yawning. I keep on swallowing.* When I read that, I felt confused. Was my grief fear? How was I supposed to know which was which?

I stop at the corner of Barrow and Hudson to look through the closed gate into the gardens. Two women are eating sandwiches on the wooden bench and talking in low voices. One of them bursts out laughing at something the other says. I start walking again, south down Hudson and then east on Leroy.

A few months ago, I started to walk home after work. It takes over an hour if I follow the shortest route, straight up along the Hudson and then cutting across Seventy-Second, but I like to stretch it out, watching the people tucked behind restaurant windows sip their first drink, then stopping for dinner myself. I started the long walks home in the middle of the summer, when most of my colleagues were leaving the office early. The older editors and writers fled at lunchtime on Fridays to make it to the Hamptons before dinner, and the younger people checked out before five to meet friends for drinks on a rooftop somewhere. I would leave a few minutes after my editor did, abandoning the cool of central air-conditioning for the sweltering heat of streets crowded with people dodging dripping air-conditioning units, sweat streaming down their necks. New Yorkers fuss endlessly about these hot months. I love feeling burned again.

At the crosswalk on Leroy and Seventh, a child pulls her father's hand and points into the road. Her eyes are wide in mute fascination. The man, talking angrily into his phone, doesn't bother to look down. He pulls his daughter in the direction they are walking, impatient to keep going, but she keeps her feet stubbornly fixed and her finger still pointing. I follow her finger and see the remains of a squirrel on the road – body flattened by a tyre, fur matted with blood, pink insides exposed. The head is still perfectly intact, eyes open. Two boys with matching shocks of red hair whizz by on skateboards, and the breeze they make moves through the animal's fur. For a moment, the squirrel looks like it is breathing again.

10.

THAILAND, Saturday, 25 December 2004

The sky is bright blue again, but the sea is still unsettled from the storm. Arielle is lying across the front of the boat, her head dangling toward the water. The waves are whispering to each other. Anurak kills the engine; the water lifts and drops the boat. Arielle sits up.

Ten feet away, something breaches and comes crashing down on the surface of the water. Eyes scan the sea. Nik and Katerina are sitting next to each other. His fingers graze her thigh. Arielle sucks in her cheeks.

Rosie, as always, is ready first. While everyone else gets their gear ready, she looks for foreign boats, but the only other vessel in sight is a liveaboard run by a diving company that operates out of Phuket.

We have been diving at the cleaning station on the reefs on

the southeast coast of the island at 8 a.m. and noon every day, except today, for the past three weeks. Mantas are opportunistic feeders – they eat when and where there is food – but they clean like clockwork. It's 3 p.m. now. We almost never dive this late, and we rarely come to the west of the island. We are outside the protected waters here.

My father and Rosie sit on the side of the boat facing us. They tip themselves backward in unison, their heads disappearing into the water before their feet do. Matthew follows a few seconds later, then Nik and Katerina from the other side of the boat. Finally, our turn. Arielle puts on her mask and bites down on her regulator. I check the water to make sure it's clear; she doesn't wait for me. I watch her disappear into the water.

The water is clear and cool, the reef is peaceful. There is not a manta in sight. Disappointment courses through me; Rosie signals patience and crosses her legs. The water holds her in place. For all her earthly ungainliness, Rosie is sheer elegance in the water. Other swimmers push and pull their way through the ocean, fighting to move forward or to stay still, but when Rosie swims, it looks like the water propels and cradles her, as if the current serves her. She is a creature made for the sea.

The delicate orange branches of a fan coral wave in the current. A pair of cleaner wrasses are trying to find a customer for their services, but no other fish is interested. Matthew aims his camera at a bluespotted ribbontail ray hunting along the seabed. I inhale and exhale slowly and tilt my head back to watch a school of snapper pass above me. Arielle swims away from me to pursue a parrotfish around the reef.

When I look back at Rosie, she is pointing into the deeper blue. Five mantas swim out of the ocean and into the shallow reef. Another five appear, then more, and more. A huge squadron. There are twenty rays, then thirty, then forty. I lose count. I've never seen so many male mantas together. We all descend and move outward to give them more room. Matthew lets himself sink until his knees hit the seafloor, then he turns his camera upward.

Soon, a male starts shadowing a young female, then he's followed by another, then another. They form a long train behind her, and she starts to put them through their paces. She accelerates and decelerates and accelerates again. The males match their speed to hers. She moves straight toward the seafloor and then explodes up toward the surface. She's testing them. She is making them dance with her, or for her. We all stare, entranced, as they soar above us. I understand, for the first time, why another venery noun for rays is a fever.

The males at the back of the train are starting to tire, the gap between each manta is growing. My oxygen is getting low, but I refuse to miss any of this. I stop moving and start taking slower, deeper breaths. Finally, the female manta slows down and the lone remaining male catches up to her. He takes her left pectoral fin in his mouth and bites down hard. A wisp of blood muddies the water around them. Once he has a good grip, he flips his body underneath hers, and they fuse together, falling slowly toward the seabed. The whole act lasts only about thirty seconds. A quick wrestling match without consent. The male swims away and the female bears her first scar.

Back on the boat, we each sit facing the sea, dazed by so much beauty. No one wants to return to life outside the water.

Katerina is the first to break the silence. "I've never seen anything like that."

"And you may never again," Rosie replies.

Arielle comes to sit next to me, resting her head on my shoulder. She's exultant and I'm forgiven. The mantas resolved our fight for us: no dive tomorrow could be better than this. Anurak, looking out at a boat on the horizon, is worrying the frayed end of his long-sleeved black sun top.

"Pen arai?" Rosie asks. What's wrong?

"Chan mai ruujak ruea lam nan," he replies. We turn to look at the boat he is talking about. I don't recognize it either.

"Let's go," my father says, before anyone else can say anything. Anurak starts the motor and we head back home.

11.

NEW YORK, Sunday, 28 October 2012

Sometimes when I am out walking, I see the earthquake here. I see it upending houses that have stood since the beginning of the last century. I see the buildings start to crack and crumble, spitting out bricks slowly, first one by one, then whole rows at a time. Only after this does the water come rushing through the streets, two storeys high, devouring everything in sight. The water comes from all sides. The Hudson and the East River rise in tandem with the Atlantic and together they sweep the streets. I feel myself floating, higher and higher, until I am looking down on the chaos from above.

When this happens, I press my eyes shut and squeeze my left wrist with my right thumb and forefinger. Only then do the streets dry, the houses settle back down, the people return to their feet.

One of the articles I had to fact-check last week (*How to Have the Best Day in the West Village*) is about the streets I'm walking through now. *After a leisurely morning stroll to admire the prewar buildings that were once home to famous artists and writers, settle down to brunch at one of the quaint little tables in the leafy courtyard of a beloved French bistro.* I had to email the author to ask which artists and writers he meant, determine whether "famous" was an appropriate adjective, ask the copyeditor if the use of "once" suggested that famous artists no longer live here, and call the restaurant to check if "French bistro" was an accurate description.

Articles about that day always include a quote from a tourist: *It was a beautiful day.* For some reason, it is important to both the survivors and the journalists to stress this. *The sky was blue*, they say, *the sun was out*. If it had been overcast, would this all have been easier? Some of these same people call it *the* wave, as if there was only one.

We didn't move to the island straightaway. My father wanted to enroll me in school and set up a bank account. My mother's parents urged him to send me to a "good school". They would send the money, they insisted. We spent two weeks in Phuket at a bed-and-breakfast run by a young Thai couple who watched us anxiously as we ate our complimentary "hot" breakfast, two fried eggs and a single slice of tomato. Every day. We emptied our plates quietly and dutifully. In those first days, my father tried not to cry, but every time I looked at him his eyes were brimming with tears. In our room, when he thought I was asleep, he sobbed and tried to muffle the noise in his pillow.

At the end of the second week, after he had found a school and a bank, we paid our bill and said goodbye to the couple. At the jetty, we were greeted by a soft-spoken fisherman whose hands and face were darkened from long days under the sun. "Mr Isaiah? Miss Marissa?" My father and I nodded together. I had learned already that I should press my hands together in front of my chest and bow slightly. He smiled at me and did the same. "Sah wah dee khrap. My name is Anurak."

Anurak led us down the wooden planks of the jetty, past boats painted with bright stripes and garlanded with long brightly coloured cloths, until we reached a simple wooden boat with no paint or cloth or awnings. He jumped in and turned to give me his hand. I put one foot gingerly into the boat and felt it sway beneath my feet. I clutched his hand tighter. He smiled at me, lifted me up off the jetty, and swung me easily into the boat. I turned to watch my father, wondering if he would need help, and saw him jump, sure-footed, and land beside me. Anurak started the engine and gestured for me to sit on the single wooden strip that stretched across the boat.

I immediately envied the way Anurak and my father walked on the boat, as if it were parked on dry land. My father sat in the prow of the boat, facing the water, with his eyes closed. He was bathed in sunlight and the water from the ocean sprayed across his face. For the first time since my mother's death, I saw his shoulders relax.

As we approached the island, we saw a large woman, barefoot in a loose flowery dress, standing on the beach, waiting for us. When we landed she gave my father a brief, tight hug and said, "I'm so sorry, Isaiah." His eyes filled again.

"Hello," she said to me. "I'm Rosie."

"Hello," I said.

"Are you hungry?"

I nodded.

"Let's get you something to eat," she said. "Matthew has been cooking all morning."

A fire engine screams past, bringing me back to the street and halting all conversation around me. A cortege of police cars and two ambulances follow, and the sound of sirens vibrates in my throat. Before the noise of the last ambulance fades, the cars that pulled over twist their wheels away from the pavement and continue north up Sixth Avenue. I start walking again and the breeze laced with the smell of rubbish gives way to still air thick with the smell of melted butter. The IFC is showing Hitchcock's *Psycho* and a documentary about the Haitian earthquake. A couple outside are arguing about which one to watch. He's in the mood for murder, he says. By the look of it, so is she.

Five men in blue jeans, neon jackets and orange safety hats are repairing the road. Four of them stand watch as one uses a machine that spits fire to evaporate water. Suddenly, with no apparent trigger, two of them are in a heated argument; the other three act as if they can't see or hear them. Another block north, a moving truck is blocking traffic and the stuck cars are united by their horns. I step into a bodega to take a break from the noise.

A small grainy television above the counter is blaring the local news. "And now, for more on the weather and the monster storm that is heading our way, here's Brad." The camera shifts to a man with blow-dried blond hair, a fake tan and an indigo suit who starts talking about how the hurricane will approach, when and where it will make landfall, what to buy, what to do, what not to do. Brad is barely able to hide his excitement. A radio playing music is competing with the television. Depending on which aisle I am in, I can hear either the mournful husky tones of Adele or the shrill warnings of the weatherman: *headed for millions of people . . . But I set fire to the rain . . . this storm is transitioning, folks . . . Watched it pour as I touched your face . . . this could be a historic first . . .*

I run my finger around the edge of a tin of condensed milk. The lady painted on the can, delicately balancing a full pail of milk on her head with one hand while she carries a second pail in her other, looks out at me seductively, a curl of red hair falling perfectly across her forehead. She is dressed for a men's magazine photo shoot. She'd never make it back home with the milk, I think, not in those clothes. I hear Arielle whisper in my ear, *What a little slut.* I nearly laugh out loud.

Arielle and I used to avoid condensed milk on weekdays, but on Sundays at the hotel, we ate fat omelettes followed by pa thong ko drowned in it. Like Anurak, Aroon, who was in charge of the station, would smile when he saw us coming. By the time we reached the counter, he would already be lowering the soft, pale dough into the vat of hot oil. Aroon was from a fishing family, but he had found work at the hotel when he was a boy and was training to be a chef. We'd watch as he lifted the golden-brown bread with tongs, shook off the excess oil, and tipped the pieces onto our outstretched plates.

If Arielle's father was away on one of his golfing holidays, we would grab a can of condensed milk from the kitchen and take it and our dangerously high piles of hot fried bread to feast in the bedroom. We traded gossip and delighted in the air-conditioning. When we had no bread left, we spooned the condensed milk straight into our mouths until we reached a state of delirium. We'd spend the rest of the morning in fits of giggles, riding high on the sugar, then crash in the afternoon.

On days when her father was at the hotel, patrolling the lobby, we would join her mother at the table where she worked in the corner of the breakfast restaurant, out of his sight line. She ate a single piece of toast before she started paying invoices and planning the grocery order for the week ahead. Arielle and I raced through breakfast so we could leave for the beach as quickly as possible. But sometimes, when her husband was away, Arielle's mother cooked for us in the evenings, even though there was no need. These were my favourite times at the hotel, the three of us eating a quiet dinner in front of the television in their suite, away from the guests. Her mother was different those nights – relaxed, quick to laugh, full of stories about her childhood in Bangkok.

I take the can of condensed milk off the shelf, check to see if anyone is looking, and slip it into my bag. Arielle looks impressed: *Have you been practising?* I shrug my shoulders slightly.

She leaves me alone only when I take a man to bed. I spend so much time alone so that I can be with her. I sleep with so many men so that I can get some time to myself. I grab a bag of sliced white bread for tomorrow, take a bottle of water from the fridge for right now, and get in line to check out.

The weatherman is picking up steam: "This is not a drill, ladies and gentlemen. This. Is. Not. A Drill. The lady in front of me clicks her tongue at the screen and opens the packet of chewing gum she hasn't yet paid for. I understand her irritation with the carelessly conducted hysteria. Every year, the weather channels warn of disaster: *This is going to be a monster storm, be prepared, this is not a joke, folks, cancel your travel plans, buy bottled water, stay at home, don't commute.* Most of the time, weathermen are boys crying wolf.

"You can see it swirling right over my shoulder here," Brad continues breathlessly. None of the weathermen and women are talking about the moon. Monday will be a full moon. The tide will be higher and the flooding worse.

When she gets to the counter, the lady says, "Two packets of Newport Lights." No hello. No please. The Yemeni man at the cash register doesn't lift his gaze from the screen as he picks the cigarettes off the shelf behind him and scans them, then a plastic bottle of orange juice and the opened pack of gum.

"Storm is coming," he says. "You want bread also? Milk?" She throws the cigarettes and gum into her bag and twists open the orange juice.

"That's what they said last year," she huffs, before she strides out.

Just wait, I think, *just wait and see*. I step up to the counter and say hello. The shopkeeper remains riveted by the news and doesn't reply, but he nods approvingly as he scans the bread and tosses it into a plastic bag. I take it out and hand the bag back to him.

12.

THAILAND, Saturday, 25 December 2004

We don't wait for the boat to dock before we leap onto the jetty and run to the hotel, weaving in and out of a pack of German tourists wearing football jerseys – KLOSE, BALLACK, LAHM. The restaurants along the beach are tackily decorated – long strings of green and red tinsel, paper cutouts of Christmas trees, sad little Santa statues – to lure in tourists who are missing home.

I feel disoriented stepping back onto the mainland after several days on the island – children shrieking, drunken laughter, the motors of taxis, the roar of speedboats, the cries of vendors selling their wares. We run until we reach the back entrance to the hotel kitchen and tumble through the swinging doors, nearly falling on the just-mopped floors. The line cooks laugh at us, then get back to work.

Daw, one of the dishwashers, knows what we have come for – he reaches into the fridge and pulls out two glass bottles of Coke. He opens them with quick snaps of his wrist and hands them over. We chug until the fizz burns our throats and we have to come up for air.

I love the ordered chaos of the hotel kitchen during mealtimes – the frenzied ballet of cooks, dishwashers and waiting staff directed by Franz, the Austrian head chef – but my favourite time to be here is now, in the gap between mealtimes when the pace is slower, the room quieter. The women – Rutna, Kwang, Suda and Ying – are preparing the fresh herbs for the day (bird's-eye chilli and lime leaves) and Franz is away for his afternoon nap. Some days, before school, I sneak in to eat khao tom for breakfast with Suda and Ying while the rest of the hotel sleeps.

The four women are sitting at a table in the corner, a wad of newspaper stuffed under one of the legs to keep it level. There is a fan trained on the table but sweat rolls steadily down their necks and arms. They are talking casually, gossiping about some woman I don't know. Their arms move like lightning, repeating movements they no longer need to think about. The sharp knives catch the light as they come down on the chillis, beheading them swiftly one by one and then slicing through the middles to reveal their seed-filled insides. They are making two piles — one for the Thais and the Indian guests, and another for the white guests who ask *Is it very spicy? I like spicy but I like to taste my food* before they order anything. For the first pile, they slice the chillis into perfect round Os. For the second pile, the knives move up and down once in a single swift movement and the chillis are left bare, stripped of every seed. Tedious work but they make it look easy.

The door to the kitchen opens and Arielle's father enters the kitchen. The four women sit up straight and stop talking. Daw starts polishing a glass, and we set our empty bottles on the counter behind our backs. Arielle's father, eagle-eyed, sees them at once and shakes his head.

"I thought you weren't coming back until next week," he says.

Arielle's face darkens, but she stays silent.

"We're just here for one night," I say politely. "We're going back to the island tomorrow afternoon." He ignores me and turns to Daw. Speaking in the bizarrely accented broken English he uses with the staff, he starts listing complaints about the lunch service.

Out of his line of sight, Arielle picks up two whole chillis from the table and offers me one. I shake my head. Before she can take a bite, I take both chillis out of her hand and give them back to Suda. Arielle's father returns his attention to us.

"Stop disturbing the staff," he says. "And put some clothes on if you're going into the lobby."

I take Arielle's hand and pull her through the back door and toward the beach.

All across the sand, fleshy European tourists are falling asleep under the midday sun, their pale skin blushing then crisping. An old man, radish purple, wakes up with a start, slowly rubs his eyes, then peels himself off the plastic deck chair. He waddles toward the water, looking for relief. A toddler nestles against his mother's body and sucks his thumb; sweat drips down her calves. A Swedish family of five who have been on holiday so long their skin is a rich umber are lying in a row, all blond and chocolate. A man selling tender coconuts walks barefoot through tourists taking photos of one another with expensive cameras. Two women sitting on mats beckon people to come get a back massage.

Everywhere, soft white sand sinks underfoot. The air pops with the crisp unlocking of drink cans. Cheeks and shoulders are starting to blister. As humans roast themselves in the sun, dark birds take turns sheltering under the shade of umbrellas.

My skin is prickling with the heat; the edges of my feet are burning. I didn't notice Arielle had left until she comes back with half a mango in either hand. My mouth starts to water when I see the fruit. I reach out wordlessly for my half – it is too hot to talk – and sink my teeth into it. Fridge-cold, perfect. The bottom of my mouth puckers, readying itself for sourness because I know mango season is long over, but the fruit is sweet. Juice trickles thickly down our chins. Both of us are ravenous after the afternoon dive. We eat to feed our hunger and soothe our disappointment at being back among the tourists.

Two six-packed boys chase each other down the beach, sending up sprays of sand with each step. We watch them as we lick the last traces of juice from our fingers. A little girl with an ice-cream cone stands entranced by the patient dance of the gulls hopping from one foot to the other.

When we were children, Arielle and I would catch jagged lime-green leaf insects and dull brown stick insects in the patches of forest near the beach and release them onto the stomachs of sleeping tourists. I was indiscriminate – drunk Australian students, young Indian honeymooners, Swedish octogenarians. Arielle was purposeful: always fat Russian men, their red skin taut over bellies round with morning beer, snoring under the midday sun as their beautiful young wives chased toddlers across the sand, their bodies so thin and tight it seemed impossible that the children were their own. I was clumsy, often almost getting caught or having to abort the mission when my victim woke up with me steps away. Arielle developed it into an art – walking quickly past the rented chairs as if eager to get to the ocean, her hand moving so quickly that I could barely see it. And, miraculously, there the creature was, perfectly perched, head up in surprise.

Arielle gets up again and I see her lift two Bacardi Breezers – one lime, one peach – from a bucket lying between a snoring couple. No one notices the theft except me. She walks back slowly, with a small proud smile, and presents me with another gift. As thanks, I open both the bottles for us with my teeth and tear open a packet of crisps I took from the kitchen. On cue, two mynah birds land nearby and watch the packet with greedy brown eyes, their lemon-yellow feet dancing closer whenever they think we aren't looking.

Arielle stands up and shakes her body so that thousands of grains of sand cascade from her stomach and legs onto the ground. The men around us start to pay attention; their wives pretend not to notice.

"Coming?"

I drain what is left in my bottle, and we swim out to the farthest buoy.

13.

NEW YORK, Sunday, 28 October 2012

It has started raining, barely, and the people on the streets are scattering for cover. They disappear into shops and pharmacies, or down the slick stairs to the subway. When I first came back to this city, I was bewildered by this behaviour. New Yorkers, normally on fast-forward through the streets, are put on pause by a light drizzle. They wait. They huddle together under awnings and at subway exits, politely ignoring the person right next to them. Suddenly, patience. *Are they crazy?* I used to think. *I cannot wait in this subway station for three days.* I feel most alien in New York, the city of my birth, when it rains. It still makes me laugh when I hear people say, *It's pouring.* I always think, *You have no idea*, and I am flooded with longing for the mesmerizing deluges of my childhood.

Most foreigners time their trips to Thailand for the weeks when the sun shines all day. Arielle and I pitied them for missing the more serious beauty of the monsoon: the loud, rhythmic beating of the rain on the sand, the way the pitch-dark sky turned white with lightning, the heart-stopping cracks of thunder. When the sky opened and the rains came, it was difficult to remember any other days. We loved diving when it rained – we would turn our bodies to face the sky and watch from below as the drops landed on the surface of the sea, silently absorbed by the water. But on most such days, we couldn't take the boat out; the sea was too dangerous, and we stayed inside, talking and reading, drawing and writing.

One stormy afternoon when we were eight, I drew the splayed legs of a giraffe and handed the paper over to Arielle. She finished the picture with the head and neck of an emu. *A gi-mu*, she announced, and we giggled. We spent the next three hours collaborating on pictures of creatures that didn't exist.

Memories like this still come to me unbidden. For months after the tsunami, my brain refused to include anyone else. I wanted to keep Arielle to myself. I couldn't stand the thought of sharing her.

. . .

In the window of a hardware store, a handwritten sign reads: ARE YOU READY FOR THE STORM? Another sign next to it says: WE HAVE BATTERIES, FLASHLIGHTS, WATER. Underneath it, in different coloured ink, someone has written, all lowercase, *no more battries*. The nail salon next door advertises a heavy discount for Mondays and Tuesdays and a special price for a ten-minute massage with your manicure. I push the door open, a bell chimes. Before the door closes behind me, the lady at the front asks what I want.

"Manicure and eyebrows."

"Gel?"

"No, just regular."

"Threading or waxing?"

"Threading."

"Okay, choose your colour."

I swirl the rotating shelves of polish and pick out a deep, dark red: Midnight in Moscow.

"Come, sit here," she says, leading me to the chair farthest away from the window. "Two minutes."

There are Bollywood posters on the wall, Bollywood songs playing from the speakers, and three different Bollywood music videos playing on three television screens. The smells of acetone and sandalwood incense mingle in the air.

Two white women getting pedicures next to each other are scrolling through their phones. The technicians are talking to each other in Nepali. One of them says something that makes all the others laugh. The woman getting her toenails painted lime green looks up from her phone as if wondering if they are talking about her, then leans over and shows her friend something on the screen.

In my first months in Thailand, I had no friends. I was the only child on the island. The adults took turns keeping me entertained and teaching me what they knew. My father taught me how to swim, first in the shallows of the mangrove forests, then in the gentle waves that lapped the main beach; Matthew showed me how to navigate the forest, how to make my own breakfast, and how to take photographs.

First, he carefully explained aperture and shutter speed and exposure. He let me practise on his fancy camera, but he insisted that I started with small inanimate objects – leaves, sticks, pieces of fruit – before I could move on to landscapes or people. Once he felt I was ready, he showed me how to take portraits, some posed, some candid. I used to photograph every guest who came to the station. Later, I mostly used Arielle as my muse. I have a box of those photographs; none of them do her justice. She is either smiling unnaturally or caught in some expression that I don't remember her ever wearing. I worry that my memories will one day be tainted by these bad photographs. I have only one video of her. She is doing a terrible impression of a posh English actor and I'm laughing so hard that the camera doesn't stay still. Matthew isn't in frame, but I can hear him laughing too. Of the hundreds of photographs of us in the ocean, none survive. They were all destroyed that day.

When Matthew was a young boy, he found an old, unused camera in the church his parents used to go to in Kochi. He started taking photos of everything – the fruit stalls on the street, his friends playing cricket, his grandmother's slippers, the trees outside their house. He was terrible at first – the pictures were unfocused, badly framed, poorly lit – and he nearly gave up. But his father told him to keep going and bought him a secondhand copy of Henri Cartier-Bresson's *The Decisive Moment*. He began to understand how to make the camera see what he saw. *I studied that book like the Bible*, he told me, *and it changed my life.*

On one of his long stints in the jungle, he fell in love with an Englishman called Jonathan who was part of a BBC crew filming a documentary about tiger cubs. They courted over cups of sweet tea by the morning fire, sat next to each other on the long drives in the jungle, and smoked beedis together at night. They had been together for less than a year when Jonathan took a quick trip back to England between shoots and had a cardiac arrest playing football at a local park. When Matthew showed up at the funeral, no one knew who he was. He left without introducing himself.

I realized only after I had left the island that what Rosie had built there was a refuge. She had taken in two broken men, each grieving his own separate loss, and had given them the space they needed to mend.

As she wipes the old polish off my fingers, the nail technician asks me where I'm from. I never know how to answer this question. Do I tell her where I was born, where I grew up, where my parents are from, where their parents are from, or where I live now? I say what I usually say when people ask.

"I thought maybe India," she says, sounding disappointed.

"Are you from India?" I ask, even though I know she isn't.

"Nepal."

"How long have you been in America?"

"Seven years."

She tells me that she has been home only once in the seven

years that she has lived here. She has an aunt who also lives in Queens, but the rest of her family is back home. She misses home. The weather, the food, her parents, her sister, her friends.

"It's too cold here," she says. She is smiling, but there is sadness in her voice.

When my nails are cleaned and trimmed, the lady covers both my hands with a hot towel and squeezes them together. This is my favourite part of a manicure – the short massage right before they start painting. I get my nails done more often than I need because I miss being touched this way.

I zip up my coat to protect my neck from the rain. Arielle stretches her arms out and turns her palms upward to catch the drops. I try to dispel her by reciting a stanza from *In Memoriam*.

> **She** *is not here; but far away*
> *The noise of life begins again,*
> *And ghastly thro' the drizzling rain*
> *On the bald street breaks the blank day.*

But this is how it is sometimes. I imagine her with me, her instead of me, what she would say, how she would look, the way her face would move. If I'm eating, or drinking, or walking, or shopping, or watching TV, she is next to me. Now, she skips past strangers on a street she's never stepped on.

When I'm by myself, I talk to her. I can carry on for a while because I know what she would say. I used to be able to finish her sentences. If I did it too many times in a row, she would say something so outrageous that we would both dissolve into laughter, breathless, giddy. But we sometimes didn't need to speak to each other at all. The twitch of an eye, the movement of an upper lip, the shrug of a shoulder was enough. She could translate the slight raise of my eyebrows into a full paragraph on what I thought about a person. My job was easier – she wore her feelings on her face.

A man in a dark suit and pink tie walks past me and comments approvingly about a part of my body.

Fuck you, I think.

"Thank you," I say.

I speak quietly, eyes to the pavement. He stops, barely a foot away from me, and says I'd look better if I didn't cover myself up with so many clothes. I don't lift my gaze, and he walks away. If men are like this with me, they would never have left her alone.

14.

THAILAND, Saturday, 25 December 2004

We float, weightless in the salty ocean, our feet occasionally bumping, until the sun sinks below the sea and turns the undersides of the clouds pink and orange. We swim slowly back to shore, picking up litter on our way – plastic bottles, a single rubber slipper, two empty cans of Red Bull, a yellow toy spade.

We towel our stomachs and arms dry. Arielle tosses her wet hair forward, sending spray across the sand. I hop on my right leg to clear the water in my right ear. We walk back to the hotel, past the restaurants serving all-day breakfast and the usual snacks for tourists, for whom bar service begins at 10 a.m. At the hotel's outdoor restaurant, a shirtless man, salmon pink and hairy, is sitting alone at a table littered with empty beer bottles and cigarette butts. As we walk past, he reaches out and wraps his thick fingers around Arielle's wrist and pulls her toward him. He is looking at her bare stomach, alcohol in his eyes, when he slurs, "How much?"

My fury is sudden and total. I am ready to rain fists down on this ugly man's bald head. Arielle says nothing, she glances down at her hostage wrist and then back up at him, her head tilted in amusement.

"How much?" he says again, insistently, anger creeping into his voice. He is old enough to be her father's father. Without saying a word, Arielle uses the fingers of her other hand to unhook his grasp.

"Bitch," he spits after us.

Smiling, she takes my hand in hers and pulls me away.

The kitchen is busy now: dinner service is in full swing, Franz is in control. He frowns slightly in our direction but doesn't break his rhythm; the staff barely register us. My hands are shaking, my face is hot with rage, but Arielle walks over to the board and points at the ticket for table 23: burger, fries and a milkshake. She rolls her eyes.

We have grown up around men like this, men who think they can touch you, hold you, own you; men who come here in droves knowing they can have a woman for a price. It isn't just lonely old men — the kind you see morning till evening with a young girl on their lap — but every kind you can imagine: teenagers on graduation trips, husbands on holiday with the whole family, teachers accompanying children on school trips.

Arielle takes an idle mortar and pestle and a bottle of ketchup to a small table in the corner of the kitchen. I follow, confused, until she opens her hand to reveal a handful of red chillis stolen from the pile, seeds included. She grinds them up slowly, with deliberation. A red stain spreads over the inside of the marble mortar. Arielle mixes the ketchup in with her finger, then checks her new concoction. There is triumph in her eyes.

"Twenty-three on deck!"

Within seconds, she tips the new ketchup perfectly into a ramekin and gets to the door before the waiter does. No one else sees her make the switch.

The man leans back when the food arrives, watching the waiter set it down on the table. He picks up three French fries with his thick fingers and dips them all into Arielle's ketchup. We stay long enough to watch him cough and splutter and choke. When I turn to look at her, her face is serious, grimly satisfied.

"Let's go," I say. I don't want her to be here when her father returns.

15.

NEW YORK, Sunday, 28 October 2012

I step through the crimson doors of the bookshop on the corner of West Tenth and Waverly and I am in a different world, warm and soothing. Faded carpets lie over the scratched wooden floor, a vase of dried flowers sits on the shelf, matching gold-and-emerald library lamps are scattered across the room. A man wearing blue jeans and a black woollen sweater is asking the older woman behind the desk for a recommendation: "A novel set in India . . . I am going there next month . . ." A thin blonde woman, leafing slowly through a Burmese cookbook, stops on a recipe for khao suey and starts studying it.

Between the new fiction and the cookbooks, there is a small

table dedicated to books about New York: the smash success with a sunshine-yellow cover about the doctor who walks everywhere, the speculative novel about the female elevator inspector, the classic about the high-society beauty who eventually dies from loneliness. I pick up the smallest book on the table and open it to the first page. *On any person who desires such queer prizes New York will bestow the gift of loneliness and the gift of privacy.* This is a man's sentence. For women, especially young women, this city gives with one hand. It is generous with the gift of loneliness, miserly with privacy. I read more: *I sometimes think that the only event that hits every New Yorker on the head is the annual St. Patrick's Day Parade.* Lucky man to have lived before the annual abyss of SantaCon.

I spend much of my time like this – in shops and movie theatres and nail salons – so I can be alone in the company of other people, but I love nowhere in this city more than this oasis in the middle of the West Village. The regulars here speak in whispers, and the staff talk to you only if you talk to them first. The shop is a sanctuary; it is a place for quiet and thinking. For the last year, I have come here at least once a week before I go to dinner by myself at an Italian restaurant a few blocks west. Sometimes I'm in and out in five minutes, sometimes I spend almost two hours. Most of the staff recognize me and smile a greeting. The curly-haired man and I have talked about books many times, but we've never exchanged names.

I stroke each of the covers of the books on the table marked STAFF FAVORITES, then start reading first lines.

> *Long ago in 1945 all the nice people in England were poor, allowing for exceptions.*

> *We had been living together for about a week when my roommate told me she had asked specifically to be paired with a girl from a world as different as possible from her own.*

> *In that place, where they tore the nightshade and blackberry patches from their roots to make room for the Medallion City Golf Course, there was once a neighborhood.*

> *The sun had not yet risen.*

I know at once: this is the book I will take home today. I keep reading. *The sea was indistinguishable from the sky, except that the sea was slightly creased as if a cloth had wrinkles in it. Gradually as the sky whitened a dark line lay on the horizon dividing the sea from the sky and the grey cloth became barred with thick strokes moving, one after another, beneath the surface, following each other, pursuing each other, perpetually.* I pick up the book and hold on to it as I continue to browse the shelves.

. . .

In the travel section, I pick up a Thai travel guide and phrase book and flip through the sections: *There are four ways of saying* you *in Thai.* This is not true, there are more than four. There is a *you*, for example, reserved just for monks, another for addressing the royal family, another for children or women much younger than the speaker.

My Thai was better than Arielle's. This was a huge source of pride for me and an even bigger source of irritation for her. She spoke it only with her mother, when they didn't want guests to understand what they were saying, and with her mother's parents when they visited; I had spent weeks when I first arrived speaking only to Anurak, while my father, Rosie and Matthew were diving. The staff at the hotel spoke to me in Thai and Arielle in English, and it drove her crazy.

Arielle's father hated it when his in-laws visited, not least because the staff responded to them with the kind of automatic deference he craved. He would insist her mother translate every word her parents said. I listened, impressed, as she revised their sentences in real time, effortlessly transforming her mother's torrent of insults and complaints into empty pleasantries. When Arielle's grandmother called her son-in-law a mediocre, lazy farang, I had to turn away before he saw my face. Arielle couldn't always keep up when her grandmother spoke quickly, but her mother knew I understood every word.

After the guidebook's list of the best beaches in the country, there is a warning: *Drownings are common.* But in all the years I spent on the beach pictured on the cover of this book, I witnessed only one drowning. I was twelve. A Scottish man got stuck in a riptide and tried to fight his way out. Arielle and I were playing on the beach when we heard the commotion. Several people were shouting and running toward the water. Two men working on the beach jumped onto a speedboat and went to rescue him, but it was too late. Parents shielded the eyes of their children as someone tried to resuscitate him. Six men helped carry the body to the road so the ambulance could take it away.

My father taught us both how to get out of a rip. *Never fight the ocean*, he said, *relax into it. Let it carry you out and then swim parallel to the shore. You'll make your way back to land easily*, he promised.

There is a whole chapter in the book on coral reefs and diving. *Thailand boasts some of the best diving sites in the world.* There are three pictures: a whale shark, a diver next to a dugong, and three clown fish. Arielle and I refused to go see the dugongs, who were assaulted by boatloads of tourists released into the water every morning. She hated that her father encouraged the tourists at the hotel to go on these trips. She would approach families as they were feasting at the breakfast buffet, their plates full of croissants and omelettes, fresh fruit and little cups of yogurt and granola, rice porridge and fried eggs. *How are you all doing today? Anything special planned?* A child would answer, as she knew they would, *We are going to see the dugongs!* She would smile at them and then launch into a diatribe about tourists ruining the habitat for dugongs. Once, she made a little boy cry by telling a story about how unhappy the dugong mothers were with the human children who were disturbing hers. The family cancelled the trip and demanded a refund. Arielle's father was furious. He banned her from the breakfast restaurant for the rest of the week.

I turn the page and my chest contracts. There is a full-page photograph of a manta soaring through the night sea. I recognize her from her spots: Andromache. The image is credited to a local wildlife photographer who Matthew knew well and I had met once. The caption reads: *Manta sightings are common on dives in the Similan Islands.* A short paragraph on the opposite page lists the threats that mantas face: overfishing, bycatch, poaching, entanglement, boat strikes, pollution, climate change, tourism and the aquarium trade. The photo isn't dated. I wonder how long before she was killed it was taken.

Last year, I found a YouTube video about a traditional Chinese medicine shop in Guangzhou that sold gill plates. In it, an undercover journalist, wearing a camera hidden in his shirt, walks around the shop. I couldn't believe the number of plates; they were from more rays than I had ever seen in my life combined. When asked what they are for, the man behind the counter promises that regular ingestion of gill plates can cure a wide range of ailments: acne, chicken pox, chronic cough, cancer, tonsillitis, fever, poor blood circulation. On the street outside the shop, the journalist asks a young woman holding a baby why she has just bought a bag of gill plates. *It helps with breastfeeding*, she tells him. In the video, white text appears below her face: *The gills of manta rays are known to contain arsenic, cadmium, and lead.*

I flip through the rest of the guidebook and stop on a page dedicated to Thai idioms involving animals.

> ### *Khii chaang jap takkataen*
> **Literal translation:** to ride an elephant to catch a grasshopper
> **Translation:** to put in a lot of effort to do something trivial
>
> ### *Chaang taay thang toa ao bai bua pit mai mit*
> **Literal translation:** A dead elephant can't be completely covered with a lotus leaf

Translation: You can't keep a really bad deed a secret forever

Nii suea pa jorakay

Literal translation: to run away from a tiger to meet a crocodile

Translation: run away from one danger to encounter another

I flip to the section titled ROMANCE and read the frequently used phrases:

> *Kiss me.*
> *I want you.*
> *Touch me here.*
> *Oh yeah!*
> *My god!*
> *That's great.*
> *Easy, tiger.*

I spare a thought for the men who read this book and plan to say "Easy, tiger" in Thai one night in Phuket.

16.

THAILAND, Saturday, 25 December 2004

The sky is black, the moon and stars tucked away, but the road is lit up with the strings of multicoloured party lights that line the front of each bar. Backpackers, escaped from their hostels, stand at high tables sipping bottles of Chang, baring their newly tanned biceps. The air smells of rum and sunblock.

We are out with a small group from school – Safia and Zara, identical twins from our year; Leo, Haruto, Cai and Imran, four boys from the football team. Most of our classmates have left Thailand for Christmas to visit their families around the world – Stockholm, Bangalore, Amsterdam, Melbourne, London, Tokyo – but, as always, a small group of us have stayed home for the holiday. The bouncer greets us as we walk into a bar where the dancing has already begun.

Arielle is wearing a short black skirt and a pale green halter top, her collarbones glittering under the lights. Leo has been staring at her shamelessly since we started drinking at Cai's house a few hours ago. He is hoping Arielle will give him some sign that she returns the interest, but so far she has taken no notice of him. She's been sulking since the night started. I look at Cai and nod slightly toward Leo. He shrugs at me as if to say: *What do you want me to do about it?*

"What do you want?" Cai asks out loud.

"Shots," Zara answers for all of us.

"Take him with you, please," I say quietly to Cai.

"Anything for you."

I laugh and push him away.

Cai and Leo go to the bar, and the rest of us join the packed dance floor. Arielle immediately starts scanning the room for her fun for the night. She's changed tack suddenly: if she had to come back here before she wanted to, she's going to make the trip worth her while.

When we first started to go to clubs, at fifteen, we were unprepared for the attention. We loved it indiscriminately at first, the slack-jawed look of men staring at our legs, but we've grown more protective of each other recently – we use each other as shields, pull each other away at certain moments or make strategic trips to the toilets. Over the past year, Arielle has started to ignore men with studied indifference. She feigns absolute focus on a single object so that, to a casual observer, she seems unaware of the eyes that follow her as she moves across a room. I know she sees everything.

Two tall blond men, dressed in matching Singha singlets, are standing in a corner of the bar, enthralled by our dancing. We enjoy our easy power over them. From the way Arielle is moving, I can tell she wants their attention. Cai and Leo return, each holding four shots of tequila and four thick slices of lime. The eight of us clink glasses, tip the golden liquid down our throats, and suck on the lime slices to chase the burn. Cai wipes a drop of tequila off my chin and kisses my cheek. I feel as if I've swallowed something hot.

Arielle sees it all. She throws her arms around me and says something. I can't hear any of the words above the music, but I know what she's asking.

"Go for it," I shout back. She wastes no time: she walks straight up to the tall men, and the three of them talk for a few minutes. Her body never stops moving to the music. She rests her hand on the shoulder of the taller one and leans in to whisper in his ear. Leo's face falls.

A large man who looks like he is in his forties starts dancing next to me. He has a creamy lilac drink with an umbrella and keeps wiping the sweat off his red forehead with the back of his other hand. He has a big tattoo of a flaming heart on his shoulder. I turn away from him and the twins form a little circle around me, but he continues to sidle up. Zara pulls me toward her and switches places with me so her body is between mine and his. He disappears into the crowd and I relax again. Arielle threads through bodies to make her way back to us.

"They're brothers. They're here for a week from Copenhagen. He said they're going to get another drink and come over here."

Flaming Heart appears again. I shake my head at him and try to wave him off. Without warning, he puts his hand around my waist and pulls me into him. This time it is Arielle's turn for fury. She flips around and looks him straight in the eye, spitting each word.

"Don't fucking touch her."

His eyes are blank from drink, his right hand stays around my waist.

"Get your fucking hands off her." She's shouting now. "If you touch her again, I'll fucking kill you." She looks slightly ridiculous, a tiny girl in the face of this inflated man, but she speaks with such seriousness that he seems to believe her. She scowls at him until he backs away.

The mood has soured. Arielle, still fuming, is standing still in the middle of the dance floor, Leo is moping at the bar, the Danish brothers have moved on to a different set of girls. Cai can see that I've had enough.

"Night market?" he shouts above the music.

"Yeah, let's get the fuck out of here."

We exit in a somber line.

As soon as we find a table, Arielle declares she doesn't want to eat so we should all go get our food. Everyone obeys at once; best to leave her alone. I wander through the stalls, trying to decide what to take back to her. I join the end of the long queue for papaya salad. Even though everyone is here for the exact same dish, the only one she offers, the som tum lady makes each order separately. We all watch as she tosses the strips of raw papaya with fish sauce, lime juice, chillis, peanuts, dried shrimp and palm sugar.

At the neighbouring stall, a man heaps green curry into round metal bowls. Across from the curry stall, a pair of boys are stupefied by a knockoff shoe store. The latest Jordans, black and gold, are on display. The younger boy shyly asks the store owner if he can try them on. When he has both shoes on his feet, he goes for a little walk to test them out. There is a spring in his step; he's full of joy.

When I get to the table, holding my papaya salad in one hand and a steaming bowl of noodles for Arielle, she is still raging. Her hands are shaking and she's gritting her teeth. No one else is back yet. They're probably staying away to let her calm down. I put the bowl down in front of her, hand her a spoon, and sit down.

"I told you we should have stayed," she says, not looking at me.

We eat our food in silence.

17.

NEW YORK, Sunday, 28 October 2012

I make eye contact with the bartender as soon as I enter. By the time the hostess has checked me in and led me to my regular seat, at the end of the bar overlooking the dessert station of the open kitchen, my old-fashioned is waiting for me. I climb onto the barstool and have my first sip.

"This is perfect."

"Thank you. What else can I get you?"

I tilt my head. My order is the same every week: an old-fashioned, the ricotta and crackers, another old-fashioned, the bucatini with pancetta and pecorino.

"Coming right up."

I come here because I like the food and the drinks and I like watching the work in the kitchen, but also because I can reliably take someone home: a man out for a work dinner with colleagues and clients, or celebrating something with a group of friends, or eating alone after a long day at the office.

One night earlier this year, while I was waiting for my pasta, a hush fell over the restaurant. Famous actors and musicians eat here regularly, and patrons typically reward them with little more than a passing glance. I turned in my stool, my legs dangling off the floor, intrigued to see who could have caused this reaction. It was a man with grey hair and dark bushy eyebrows standing behind two impeccably dressed women, one older, one younger, both dressed entirely in black. I recognized him from the papers: the French politician who had been arrested in New York for raping a hotel maid. The prosecutors had dropped the charges that morning and he had come to celebrate his victory with his wife and daughter over a fine Italian meal. The conversation in the room only started up again when they were tucked safely away in the private room upstairs.

The bartender starts to shake another cocktail. Arielle jumps onto the counter and starts playing with a wineglass. The bartender has dark skin and strong arms tattooed with constellations of stars. An order for three whiskey sours comes in. The bartender's muscles ripple under the strain of shaking cocktails; the stars look like they are moving against the night sky. The bartender works here four nights a week and is a freelance photographer by day. It's mostly weddings and bat mitzvahs – boring jobs that pay well – but I've seen some beautiful black-and-white portraits of strangers on city streets. After the waiter collects the drinks, the bartender and I pick up our debate from last week: which teams have the best chance of making the NBA finals this year, and who is going to be MVP. Another drink order interrupts us.

Across the counter from me, a pastry chef carefully dusts icing sugar over a round cake. She cuts it into eight perfect pieces, places each on a separate plate, and then spoons hot bursting raisins in a golden syrup and a dollop of freshly whipped cream over each slice. Four waiters appear and whisk the plates away. A table of businessmen, several bottles of wine down, are laughing too loudly behind me. One of them cheers as the cake arrives. At the table next to them, a man and his teenage daughter sit in awkward silence. His phone rings, he answers, and she, relieved, picks up her phone to start texting.

In our first year on the island, when I was seven, my father put me to sleep at night by telling me stories about the ocean from around the world. He told me about Poseidon, the Greek god of the sea and earthquakes; Ran, the Norse sea goddess who captured seafarers with a net, her husband, Aegir, and their nine daughters who personify the waves; Atargatis, the Syrian goddess who flung herself into a lake after her lover died and was transformed into a mermaid; and Sedna, the Inuit goddess of the sea and marine animals, who so angered her father that he took her out to sea in his kayak and threw her overboard.

Several years later when a visiting Japanese biologist told me about Isonade, the sharklike sea creature with a huge tail covered in barbs that lived off the coast of Nagasaki, I started craving stories about monsters. My father refused at first but then gave in to my pleading. He revised the stories, however, giving the monsters of the ocean backstories, reasons for their hunger and fury. In his retelling, Scylla had been mistreated, Charybdis misunderstood. When I read *The Odyssey* myself, I was surprised not to recognize my father's Scylla in Homer's monster. (I liked "wine-dark sea", though, a truer description of the ocean than any other I had read.)

A journalist from Australia, hearing how much I loved stories of the gods, left me a copy of *Metamorphoses*. Arielle picked it up during a storm one day and didn't stop reading, even when the rain stopped. Medusa, she decided, was her monster of choice.

By the time we were teenagers, there was a prize – the last chocolate biscuit – at the station for the visitor who could tell the scariest sea story. People often tried to retell old myths: the Biblical dragon in the sea, the Kraken, the Danish sea monk.

"I have one," said a quiet oceanography graduate student from Cambridge one year.

"Go ahead," said Rosie.

He told the story of the scientists on the first real oceanographic expedition. Two drownings, one suicide, the other two mad. Rosie handed him the biscuit and he unwrapped it proudly.

I'm only a few pages into *The Waves* when a man appears at my elbow. I look at him and then look back down at my book.

"Hey, I've been watching you all night."

"Oh," I say. I don't lift my eyes from the page.

"Can I get you a drink?"

"I'm all set." I tap my glass. "Thanks so much."

The bartender understands me well enough by now to know when to leave me to it and when to intervene.

"Can I help you, sir?"

The man ignores the bartender and slips his hand under my

shirt and onto the small of my back. He rests it there, this stranger.

"What can I help you with, sir?"

I start reading the labels of the bottles of gin behind the bar. Arielle shuffles to the left so I can see them better.

"Would you like another drink?"

The man's hand is still on my back.

"What would you like? I can bring it to your table."

I look up at the man again. He looks at me with longing; I feel pity. I look away again until he finally shrugs and leaves. The other men at his table are laughing at him when he sits back down. The man at the next table is now loudly berating the person he is talking to on the phone; his daughter looks embarrassed.

The bartender asks if I'm okay. I nod and return to Virginia Woolf.

I left school early one day in eleventh grade because I had stomach cramps. When I couldn't find any Panadol in the bedroom Arielle and I shared, I crossed the small courtyard that separated our room from her parents' suite. I knocked on the glass sliding doors but no one answered, so I let myself in.

I was at the door to the bedroom before I realized that Arielle's mother was actually there. She was sitting silently at her dresser. There was a deep purple-blue bruise on her cheek, and she was quietly mixing liquid foundation with a brush. She looked up, and we made eye contact through the mirror.

"Please," she said, Arielle's proud and graceful mother, pleading as if she were the child and I the adult. "Don't tell her." I took the brush from her trembling hand, and she turned around to face me. I started painting her cheek, each stroke disappearing another layer of blue and purple. When I was done, she turned to check her face in the mirror.

At the entrance to the kitchen, two barbacks are polishing wineglasses – they hold each one to the light to check for marks and then polish again and again, until each glass is pristine. The kitchen is busy: frying, dicing, chopping, boiling, searing, glazing. A line cook slices radishes into paper-thin circles. His hand slips and the sharp knife slides into the top of his finger. Arielle winces. The white of the radishes turns dark with blood.

As I'm finishing my pasta, I catch the eye of a man sitting alone at the other end of the bar. Arielle melts away. I hold his gaze until he stands up and comes to me. I feel in total control; I know I can bend him to my will. As he introduces himself, I close my book. The bartender knows not to interrupt this time. In less than ten minutes, we both ask for our checks. I thank the bartender and tell her I'll see her next week.

Monday

Wave crashing down on wave, and thunder rolling
Sea piles on sea as if to reach the sky,
The hanging pall of clouds is wet with spray.
Here the waves take the colour of the sand,
Swept from the deep, here black as Styx they swirl,
There flat and white they hiss in sheets of foam.

Ovid

What words are these have fall'n from me?
Can calm despair and wild unrest
Be tenants of a single breast,
Or sorrow such a changeling be?

Alfred, Lord Tennyson

We are at a fish market. The light has the quality of morning, but the air is already hot and thick. Tinny speakers play classical instrumental music as vendors hawk their wares. Motorcycles weave between stalls selling barramundi, squid, octopus, eels, prawns, crabs. Small fish lie tessellated in woven baskets lined with palm leaves and ice. Big fish are laid whole on bare wooden tables. Plump bellies and orange fins stand out in the sea of white flesh and silver scales.

You move from stall to stall, talking to the vendors. I trail a few steps behind. Rows of glassy dead eyes stare up at me. Two small children are playing with a deflated football underneath the tables. At one stall, three women in matching red aprons sit on plastic stools, using razor blades to descale fish and talking as the scales drift slowly to the ground by their feet, sometimes catching in the breeze. One woman tells a joke and the other two shake with laughter. At the stall next to them, a man rhythmically guts fish, his movements matching the music. He tosses each to the next table where a woman catches it and fillets it with clean strokes. Another woman packs the fillets into clear plastic bags and closes them with elastic bands. Blood pools in the bottom corners of the bags.

I realize I can't see you anymore. I start calling your name, over and over, but I can barely hear myself over the vendors. Something is wrong. I start to move faster, working my way backward, retracing our steps. A crowd has formed around the stall selling octopus. I push my way to the front. You are face up on the table, naked. People are bidding on different parts of your body. *Thigh! Shoulder! Ribs! Eyeballs!* A woman with a butcher's knife is poised over you. I push through the crowd and grab your hand. I try to pull you off the table. You turn to look at me and the knife slices through your neck.

18.

NEW YORK, Monday, 29 October 2012

I wake slick with sweat. I have to rub my hands against my thighs until I can no longer feel her fingers between mine. I cup my hands around my mouth and scream into them. For a long time, it was always the same nightmare: I am back in the wave. Just memory, no embellishment: swift black water laying claim to everything and everyone. Then last year, for a few weeks, I dreamed of the two of us back home by ourselves – swimming in the mangroves, circling the northern tip of the island in our kayaks at dawn, reading novels in the tree house. But this week it's been a different nightmare every night, each one wilder and weirder than the one before.

The man asleep beside me thinks he knows my name. He moaned it into my ear last night – *Tess, Tess, Tess* – before he fell asleep. I reach out and touch his cheek. He's as beautiful now as he was last night. Dark, curly hair, smooth skin, soft eyelashes, exhausted body. He looks like Odysseus washed ashore. But I am no Nausicaa, I have no desire to claim him as my own. Let the faithless man return to his faithful wife.

The man starts to stir; I slip into the living room of the hotel suite and put the kettle on. As I wait for the water to boil, I go to my coat, hanging on a hook by the door, and pull out the chillis wrapped in tissue. I take a small bite of one.

I draw the curtains to reveal floor-to-ceiling windows that overlook the river. We are ten blocks north of the restaurant, on the western edge of the island. The sky is grey, the water dark and rough. Today is the day. The heat from the chilli rises up my face. I close my eyes and inhale and exhale until I hear the kettle click off.

I pour hot water in slow, even circles over the stale ground coffee and watch tiny oil rainbows bubble to the top. I hold the bitter liquid on my tongue till it scalds, then I swallow. A copy of the *Nicomachean Ethics* lies on the marble coffee table. Yesterday's *Financial Times* is wedged inside as a makeshift bookmark.

In my sophomore year of college, I grew infatuated with a boy in our required political philosophy class: Plato, Aristotle,

Descartes, Hobbes, Locke, Kant, Hume, Mill, Wollstonecraft. He had slim hips and strong arms, and he studied in the sun-filled reading room on the second floor of the library. My cheeks would flush as soon as I saw the cobalt blue of his favourite sweater. We flirted by leaving each other messages hidden in the wings of origami swans – *Gone for a muffin. Don't leave before I get back* – and by sharing notes about *Leviathan* and *On Liberty*. But like every other boy and man I've been with, I could see him only through her eyes. I thought: *She would have been friends with him.* I wondered: *Would he have preferred her?* I pictured the three of us studying together.

I remove the newspaper from *Ethics* and start reading. A sentence has been underlined with a thick black pen: *Again, they who act on compulsion and against their will do so with pain; but they who act by reason of what is pleasant or honourable act with pleasure.* I flip forward to a section in Book IX that I have read so many times I know it by heart: *For not many at a time become friends in the way of companionship, all the famous Friendships of the kind are between* two *persons: whereas they who have many friends, and meet everybody on the footing of intimacy, seem to be friends really to no one except in the way of general society.* In a class on nineteenth-century novels I took the semester after I read Aristotle, the professor asked: *What is* Frankenstein *about?* Hands shot into the air. The professor wrote each answer on the blackboard in capital letters: *MONSTERS, JUSTICE, EGO,*

AMBITION, PROGRESS, SCIENCE, CITIZENSHIP. When there were no more hands left, I raised mine. *I think it's about friends.* The professor stared at me for a few seconds, nodded, and then turned her back and slowly added *FRIENDSHIP* to the list on the board.

When we finally made our way down the list to friendship, the class took turns talking about the strength of Victor's relationship with other men: Clerval, Walton, the creature. One boy kept using the word *homosocial*. Another boy, with his computer open in front of him, said, *The word "friendship" appears twenty-six times in the novel.* I didn't say anything, but I had meant Elizabeth and Justine. I pick up the pen on the table, underline my favourite sentences, and put the Aristotle back as I found it.

I sometimes decide whether I'm going to sleep with a man based on what is on his bookshelves. A month ago, a man I had gone on two dates with pressed a weathered copy of *Portnoy's Complaint* into my hands and told me that it would really help me understand him. When I didn't say anything in response, he added that he thought it would make me a better person. Two weeks ago, I went home with a man who didn't have any books in his three-bedroom town house. Not a single one. I realized, too late, this might be worse.

The man emerges from the bedroom; his white shirt is starched, his black shoes are polished. (I think: *She would have hated him*.) He comes up behind me and kisses my neck. I tilt my head back and close my eyes. I turn, slip my hand under his shirt, and run my hands across the smooth unbroken skin of his chest. He takes a fountain pen from his shirt pocket and asks me to write my number on a notepad embossed with the name of the hotel. I write down a fake number and hand him the sheet of paper. He folds it, puts it in the front pocket of his briefcase, and tells me I can stay in the room as long I like.

"Bye, Tess."

Goodbye.

As soon as he is gone, I turn on the television – EAST COAST PREPARES FOR MASSIVE STORM – and mute it immediately. CNN is showing a view of the hurricane from space. I drink my coffee and watch white swirls move across the screen. On the ticker tape at the bottom of the screen, news items scroll by: STOCK MARKET TO CLOSE AHEAD OF SANDY; HURRICANE SHAKES UP PRESIDENTIAL CAMPAIGN; GIANTS SWEEP TIGERS; CREW ABANDONS STORM-RAVAGED HMS BOUNTY; SANDY POSTPONES ANNA KARENINA PREMIERE; DEADLY CAR BOMBINGS ROCK DAMASCUS. The news programme is briefly interrupted by an ad for the American Red Cross. They are already appealing for donations and putting out a call for volunteers. I type the web address that flashes across the screen into my phone and click on the button to volunteer. There are plenty of choices: you can be part of the Disaster Action Team ("if you are team oriented and want to make a difference"), or a shelter volunteer ("when disaster strikes and people are displaced from their homes, you can be their shelter in the storm") or a blood donor ambassador ("the special attention you would provide helps create a favorable impression that encourages ongoing donor support").

After the tsunami, the Thai government refused foreign aid, but they put out a call for forensic experts from around the world. We were joined by men and women – Brits, Americans, Swedes, Australians, Germans – who came to help plan and manage. Disaster specialists. They were hardworking, efficient, organized. Their minds and bodies were with us, but I understood quickly that they had learned to keep their hearts away. I didn't blame them. I wonder how many of them will be summoned here this week.

When the news programme returns, someone has edited the banner: EAST COAST BRACES FOR APOCALYPTIC STORM. Most people use the word *apocalypse* as if it is a synonym for *catastrophe* or *cataclysm* or *disaster*, but the literal meaning of the word is closer to *revelation*. It is from the Greek *apokaluptein* – to uncover, disclose, reveal. This, it seems to me, is the right word for what happened on that day eight years ago. The water stripped everything bare, denuded the land, unmasked the earth.

The programme cuts from a still image of the front page of

yesterday's paper (HURRICANE DRIVES TOWARD NEW YORK WITH DEADLY FURY) to a reporter interviewing a parent ranting about the school closures. "They gave us no warning," she is saying, directly to the camera, ignoring the reporter. Back in the studio, the anchorman confirms that the city has shut down the subway. He encourages people to get home by early afternoon at the latest. The Red Cross ad plays again.

In Thailand, the international aid workers played the BBC on portable radios: *At least two Palestinians were killed when an Israeli aircraft fired a missile at the Khan Younis refugee camp in the Gaza Strip . . . Reports confirm that the death toll of the Indian Ocean has exceeded two hundred thousand . . . The world's tallest skyscraper has officially opened in Taipei . . .* As they wiped sweat off their foreheads with the back of gloved hands and chatted casually about common acquaintances, I realized that we would become dinner party fodder for them in a few years. Someone would ask them about the worst place they'd been to, they would pause for a few seconds and say, *Probably Thailand, after the tsunami.*

The woman who was in charge of cataloguing the bodies was German. She had blonde hair that she kept tied in a pristine ponytail, and bright blue eyes. She was a model of efficiency and patience. One afternoon, my stomach let out a long low growl as I was stacking wooden coffins and she looked at me sternly and said, *When is the last time you ate?* Her English was clipped but perfect. I shrugged. *Answer me*, she insisted. *How long has it been since you've eaten?* She tapped her white rubber boots against each other. *I don't want to take breaks*, I said stubbornly. *You will be no use to me if you collapse*, she said, holding out a banana. I sat down obediently and ate it.

I switch off the television, find a clean, soft T-shirt in the man's open suitcase, and put it on (inside out, to hide the logo of his law firm) over my jeans. I tuck my shirt from yesterday into my bag and let the door click shut behind me. On my way out of the hotel, a bald doorman with shiny cheeks smiles broadly at me and says, "Stay safe out there today."

On the street, an older couple with several large suitcases and a white fluffy dog are blocking the pavement. Their tiny dog will not stop barking. No amount of petting or treats will calm her down. A woman in a long skirt, drooping under the weight of supermarket bags, is shouting at her children to stay out of the street. A gust of wind lifts her skirt above her knees. A few drops of rain land on my face. A black Mercedes pulls up in front of the older couple and the driver gets out to help with the luggage. Storekeepers are taping glass windows with a series of uneven crosses. There is not a pigeon in sight.

My phone buzzes in my pocket. It's an email (subject line: *Today*) from Safia. I haven't seen her for two years. The email signature bears the name of the London law firm where she works. *Marissa, I'm in New York for work. Sorry I didn't write earlier. It was supposed to be a two-day trip and I had morning-to-night meetings both days, but I'm stuck here because of the storm. I'm staying at the Soho Grand. Come for a drink later? S.* The hotel is only a thirty-minute walk away. I write back immediately and say I'll meet her in the lobby in two hours. A young woman outside a bodega is wrestling with her regal Great Dane. It is whining, barking, refusing to move. The disquietude of the dogs, the silence of the birds: the storm really is coming.

19.

THAILAND, Sunday, 26 December 2004

"Come look at the sky," Arielle whispers.

I open my eyes to look at my watch. It is so early that the fishermen will still be taking their boats out into the open ocean. I groan; my head is heavy from the alcohol. Arielle pulls back the curtain to reveal the world outside. The sun has not yet risen but the soft bellies of the clouds are streaked with pink. I turn away.

"Marissa. Come on." She pulls at my blanket. "Come watch the morning with me." I refuse to move. "Why don't you ever do what *I* want?" I turn to answer but she has already slipped away through the screen door.

. . .

When I wake again, it is to the sound of howling. The pain in my head sharpens. I turn to see if the noise has woken Arielle too, but her side of the bed is empty and I remember that she left. My watch tells me that a couple of hours have passed. The screen door is slightly open. Just outside, a dog is moving maniacally in circles, howling loudly as he spins. I have never heard an animal make a noise like this: he's anguished, almost delirious. I crouch down, reach out my arm, and call to him softly. He approaches me, still howling. I try to stroke him but he will not be consoled. He takes the sleeve of my shirt in his mouth and tries to pull me. I shake him free but he tries again. I yank my arm away. He stares at me, his eyes pleading, howls again, then speeds away toward the gate that leads to the road behind the hotel, away from the sea. I follow him. Light is seeping into the sky, thick bands of red, orange and yellow are replacing the soft pinks and purples of the dawn.

On the road, sleepy shopkeepers are opening their shutters: one hangs long lines of T-shirts and hats from hooks on the ceiling, another is arranging green and yellow bodyboards on the pavement. Fruit vendors are organizing mangoes, durians, mangosteens, lychees and star fruit into neat piles. A woman is slicing and packaging guavas. Men are sitting on motorcycles eating their breakfast. There is a line in front of the cha yen cart; the seller pours the bright orange tea over ice and his customers gratefully accept their first dose of caffeine of the day. The dog is nowhere to be seen. I look to the roadside restaurant where a pack of stray dogs usually sleep and loiter in the mornings. It is deserted.

An elephant with a young girl on her back comes trundling down the main road. The barefoot mahout strolling alongside them is wearing a faded red hat embroidered with the insignia of an English football club – a mythical white bird standing tall holding a branch in its beak. One of the girl's slippers falls off her foot, and the mahout steps forward to catch it. The girl holds on to the other slipper with determined toes. Her parents are taking photos from the street, trying to make her smile. The girl is too enthralled with her position to pay them any attention. She waves to the people below as if she is a queen; the guava lady waves back. Three cars form a patient line behind the elephant while motorcycles pass her on the outside.

It is too quiet. I look up at the trees and see that they are bereft of birds. I join the end of the cha yen queue, hopeful that caffeine might fix my headache. One of the women who works at the front desk of the hotel is two people ahead of me. "Mai mii nok loei," I say to her. She looks confused.

"Listen." I keep speaking in Thai, pointing up at the branches. "The birds are gone." She listens to the silence, but then it is her turn to order. The man between us turns back to me and tells me he noticed the absence of the birds too.

Suddenly, the elephant stops in the middle of the road and won't go a step farther. The mahout taps the animal's hind leg. The elephant's ears flap widely, her tail lifts and stays horizontal. The mahout talks to the animal in a loud, firm voice, but she refuses to move. The elephant raises her trunk, trumpets urgently and then makes a sound like she is crying. The mahout looks perplexed; the parents look frightened; the girl looks strangely calm. The elephant bows her head and takes off in the opposite direction, nearly trampling the cars. Mahout and parents chase in her wake. The street is frozen in surprise. One of the motorcycle riders says that the animal must have gone mad. I leave the stunned shopkeepers behind and follow the narrow path to the beach.

The water is turquoise. The sky is aquamarine. The sand is a soft ivory.

20.

NEW YORK, Monday, 29 October 2012

The clouds lower and the drizzle becomes rain. I step into a gourmet supermarket on Sixth Avenue; panic shopping is in full swing. The woman in front of me has filled her basket with glass bottles of water, canned chickpeas and large bags of grapes. A man in a plaid shirt is loading up on luxuries: a jar of caviar, a tub of Castelvetrano olives, a wheel of triple-cream cheese, a box of assorted macaroons, Luxardo cherries. In the next aisle, a young couple is hunting for ingredients for a Turkish feast. He is reading the items out loud – labneh, pine nuts, dates, pomegranate molasses, sumac – and she is searching the shelves.

A few years ago, I went to Turkey in December; I thought if I went to a country she had never stepped foot in that maybe I could escape her. I roamed the busy, dusty streets alone: I plucked tiny, sour plums off street carts, I ate simit and drank black coffee sweetened with cubes of sugar at a table on the pavement, I pretended to want a carpet in the bazaar, I tried every type of baklava at a sweet shop, I watched the sun sink behind the Bosporus. When water makes you think of someone, there is no escaping them.

An older woman is picking up a grapefruit one at a time and weighing each in her hands. People keep pushing her as they barge past; she is completely unfazed. I dip my hand into a mound of cranberries and let them slip through my fingers. I feel exhausted. A woman dressed in tight yoga pants, a white crop top, and a black baseball hat asks a teenage store clerk in faded Jordans where to find the sauerkraut. He looks bewildered. "The what?"

"Never mind," she huffs and walks away.

There is a line at the fish counter. (The store is famous for fish.) A woman in a fur coat asks for two lobster tails and four wild stone-crab claws.

"You're lucky," the fishmonger says to her as he wraps them. "These are the last four."

A man in a felt hat asks how much for a pound of wild scallops, but when he hears the price he leaves without another word. The next customer in line picks up a wood-handled oyster knife and orders two dozen Wellfleets.

Little placards offer short descriptions of each fish. The butterfish, caught wild in the Atlantic, are *alluringly delicate and astonishingly versatile*. The fluke, native to New England waters, is *perfect for seafood novices*. The New Zealand red snapper, straight from the southwestern Pacific, is *a feast for all the senses*. I wonder about the person who writes the copy on these placards, and the adjectives they must collect: *mild, delicate, buttery, sweet, rich, velvety, meaty, plump, juicy, earthy, tender*. I remember that I need to file the Skeleton Coast copy before the end of the day.

A man with a cane is debating between buying three whole black cod, a whole striped bass, or swordfish steaks. *A lap of cod, a fleet of bass, a flotilla of swordfish*, Arielle recites in my ear. The fishmonger suggests branzino and explains that it was flown in from Italy that morning. "We won't have this again for a while," he adds, gesturing outside. The man agrees to the branzino and listens attentively as the fishmonger tells him exactly how to cook it: salt, olive oil, lemon. "You don't need anything else for fish this good."

For months afterward, the fishermen couldn't sell anything. Rumours spread that the fish were feeding on corpses at the bottom of the ocean. People who had eaten fish every day of their lives suddenly couldn't stand the sight of it. Some fishermen stopped going out. They went back to work only when the tourists returned. For weeks afterward, every time I swallowed, I could taste the sea.

A little girl sitting in the front of a shopping cart asks her father if they can get a pumpkin. He says yes, and her face breaks into a wide smile. She points out which one she wants and insists on cradling it in her lap while they continue shopping. She is wearing a yellow dress emblazoned with the redheaded mermaid princess.

I was too embarrassed to tell Arielle that one of the first reasons I knew we would be friends was that I loved that cartoon mermaid. I never confessed that I knew every word to every song in that movie. When I was little and my parents went away, my grandparents played me the video, again and again, to show me where they were.

Near the cashier there is a table piled high with Halloween treats and decorations. Pumpkin chocolate, pumpkin lanterns, paper pumpkins, plastic pumpkin buckets for pumpkin-flavoured candy. There are black paper bats, a box of glow-in-the-dark eyeballs, mini skull candles, big skull candles and candles shaped like human hands, a wick on each finger. As the hand melts, the fingers drip blood. *A great conversation starter*, the packaging promises.

Some details about the aftermath of that day that none of the reports included: mixed up in the wreckage, between the bodies and the remains of houses and the wrecked cars, were broken strings of Christmas lights, pieces of silver tinsel, cardboard candy canes, red tree ornaments. The sight of tinsel still makes the insides of my eyelids hot.

Before the end of the first day, the hospitals ran out of space. The monks offered their temple as a makeshift morgue. By the time I got there, it was almost full: rows and rows of bodies lined up along the cement floor. The monks asked those of us who were still searching to help them. They divided us into two teams: some to organize the corpses already there, the rest to fetch the bodies newly washed ashore.

We tucked hair behind ears to make faces visible, we rearranged limbs so they lay straight, we kept enough space between feet and heads to allow survivors to walk between the bodies. Every time we thought we might be done, the team of fetchers brought new bodies. The corpses were black and swollen, grotesque. The monks offered us blue hospital masks but the smell seeped through the thin paper and invaded our nostrils and mouths.

When tissue decomposes, amino acids break down and produce the chemicals putrescine and cadaverine. On their own, each has a unique and awful odour. When they mix together, the stench defies description.

When the temple ran out of space, we had to decide if we should stack bodies on top of one another or line them up outside. Soon, we had to do both. My back ached from all the bending and lifting; sweat rolled off my arms and legs. Above us, helicopters lifted the living from sea to sky. As I heaved bodies along the beach, I kept thinking that Arielle would have been better at this than me: stronger, fitter, more resourceful.

A woman carrying a bloated body with me started hyperventilating and retching. A monk with a pink scarf tied around his face escorted her away. I tried not to swallow for as long as I could: I kept my mouth closed and ran my tongue along my gums and teeth for moisture. When I finally succumbed, I felt as if I had ingested flesh. After one of the body collectors saw me crouch down to spit for the fourth time in ten minutes, he put his hand on my shoulder and said, *You must inhale deeply*. I looked at him, horrified. He nodded and showed me how. Inhale, exhale. Inhale, exhale. *Five times*, he said. He raised the fingers on his right hand one at a time to draw each breath out. His chest rose and fell. I hesitated, then copied him, filling my lungs with putrid air. By the fourth breath, the smell was gone. I turned to thank him but he had already gone back to work.

On the second day, someone handed out scraps of cloth dipped in Tiger Balm to the people who had come looking for their relatives. They held the clothes to their noses as they walked through the grid of decomposing bodies and lifted bloated arms and legs. Instead of faces, they looked for jewellery and scars, tattoos and birthmarks. *Her ring matches mine*, a husband said about his wife, holding a thin black ring above his head for all of us to see. *She has a star-shaped birthmark on her right calf*, a man said about his daughter. *He has our children's initials tattooed on his chest*, a woman said, staring blankly at the sea of bodies. A monk asked her quietly to tell us their names so we knew which letters to look for. Someone found the star-shaped birthmark. We all stopped as the man picked up the body and carried it up the beach. He took it to the entrance of the temple and laid it down by the feet of the monk. *This is my daughter.*

By the third day, most of us had stopped thinking about the smell. We only remembered when we left the temple each evening, and people recoiled when we went near them. I had to throw away all the clothes I wore during those days; no amount of washing could make them clean.

A few people are crowding around a makeshift table that has been set up next to the Halloween display. A small sign reads: HURRICANE MUST HAVES. There are torches, lanterns, can openers, matches and batteries of various sizes. There are only two candles left, and a man sweeps both into his basket. The woman next to him lets out a grunt of irritation. She takes two packs of batteries, a torch and a box of matches, and then resigns herself to the Halloween candles. She takes five big skulls and three hands. I pay for a bottle of coconut water, but not for the two mini skulls I slipped into my pocket, and step back outside.

The rain is picking up. The sky is darkening. The streets are starting to empty.

21.

THAILAND, Sunday, 26 December 2004

Across the beach, older couples and sleepy parents are settling into their deck chairs for the day. A man with a heart monitor strapped across his chest runs on sand still wet from the morning high tide. Three massage ladies are arranging cushions on thin mattresses while a fourth gives an older woman a foot massage. A young couple is lounging on a large striped towel. She is face down, her bikini top unclasped; he is sitting up with a book in one hand while he caresses her bare back with the other. No one seems to notice the strange silence.

Arielle is standing ankle-deep in the water, her eyes fixed on the sea. I follow her gaze: a few miles away, a line of fishing boats bobs slowly up and down. A woman with a baby strapped to her stomach walks up the beach. The baby is wearing a floppy pale pink sun hat. Her legs are dangling free but her toes are clenched so hard they are almost wrapped under her feet. She tilts her little head sideways to look up at her mother and the hat slips off her head. The woman catches it, puts it back on the baby's head, and fastens the elastic strap around her chin. A little girl and her littler sister are combing through the sand for shells. The older girl is holding at least ten shells; the younger one is empty-handed. She looks on the verge of tears. Their parents, deep in conversation, pay them no attention.

When I reach Arielle, I touch her elbow. She doesn't alter her gaze.

"Something is wrong," she says, her voice low and troubled. I step closer to her and the water reaches my calves. The sea, usually so gentle here, tugs hard at my feet. I tell her about the elephant, then about the dog. I make her listen to the silence of the birds.

"Something is wrong," she says again. I leave her and walk back up the beach. A boy in an electric-blue swimsuit is building a sandcastle. Dark freckles cover his pale cheeks. His parents are nowhere to be seen. A few feet away, a man in tiny white swimming trunks is lying down on the sand. His legs are pressed together, his arms spread wide, his eyes closed: a perfect crucifix.

. . .

"Look!" Arielle half shouts. "Marissa, look!"

The sea is pulling swiftly away from us, revealing metres and metres of sand that we have never seen before. The boy abandons his castle and chases after the retreating water. The couple stand up together. The massage women start pointing at the ocean. The sound of the waves lapping the sand is gone. Only human noises remain: the idling engines of cars and motorcycles, tourists exclaiming at the departing sea. We have never seen the ocean behave like this. Pink and orange corals stand exposed on the seabed. The woman takes her baby out of the carrier so she can show her. Arielle and I walk out onto the seabed as the water continues to recede. In seconds, the bay is almost entirely drained.

"See the fish!" shouts the girl, dropping all her shells.

"Fish!" her little sister repeats proudly. They are right: the sea has left so quickly it has forgotten the fish. Hundreds of them are flapping on the sand. All around us, men, women and children rush forward and start picking them up and throwing them back to the ocean. The baby giggles at the fish as they fly through the air.

"We need to leave," I say.

"What?" Arielle is about to pick up another fish.

"We need to move away from the water."

The roar of an engine fills the air. The noise is so loud, it is almost deafening. We turn our heads upward to find the plane: the sky is bright and empty. We look back down. The sea on the horizon lifts into the sky and slingshots back toward us as a black wall.

The massage women start shouting to everyone to get off the beach. Parents shriek and grab their children.

"Run," someone shouts. "Run!"

Everyone is screaming and running up the sand except the little boy in the electric-blue swimsuit. He has a fish in his hand, as if he is about to launch it, but fear has turned him rigid. The man with the heart monitor scoops him up and bounds up the beach. I turn to start running, but Arielle doesn't move.

"Let's go!" I scream at her.

"Arielle! Come on!"

She seems not to hear me. She stands tall, her eyes on the crest of the wave, her shoulders relaxed. The sea swallows her whole.

22.

NEW YORK, Monday, 29 October 2012

The streets are emptying. Most of the stores are shuttered and locked, but the sign in the door of a small paint shop stills reads OPEN. Inside, I don't see anyone, but soft pop is playing over the speakers and the lights are still on. An entire wall is covered with square patches of every colour imaginable. I move closer to the reds and pinks so I can read the names: Charisma, Heartthrob, Valentine, Rosebud, Proposal, Hot Lips. One of them, Coral Dust, warm and muted, bears no resemblance to the magenta reefs we knew so well.

I move on to the neutrals: Reflection, Gossamer Veil, Tinsmith, Useful Gray, Ethereal Mood, Overcast. I pause at Elephant Tusk and think about that elephant and the little girl whose life he might have saved. Where is she now? Was she orphaned? I can still see the steady calm in her eyes before the elephant galloped away. Not a single animal that was free to move lost its life that day. As humans walked toward the retreating ocean, readying ourselves for slaughter, snakes slithered uphill, cats and dogs climbed to higher floors, birds, monkeys and deer moved themselves to safety. I stroke a swatch that I like: Gray Owl.

"I like that one," says a cheery voice from behind. I jump. The young store clerk smiles at me widely – the pink (Hot Lips) elastics on his braces clash with the green (Feel the Energy) of his name tag. The white (Bride to Be) letters read: DANNY.

"It's very calming," Danny continues. Arielle, who is standing next to him, says, *Ask him if there are any other endangered species to choose from.*

"I like it too," I reply. "But I'll keep looking. Thank you." He looks slightly hurt at being dismissed so quickly. "Let me know if I can help you with anything. I'm closing in ten minutes."

Once he's gone, I shift my attention to the blues. I try to count how many names refer to water (Nautilus, Drizzle, Ebbtide, Sea Star, Waterfall, Intercoastal Green, Aegean Teal, Florida Keys Blue, Caribbean Cool, Jamaican Aqua, Dolphin's Cove) but soon lose track.

In my first year back in New York, the world looked muted

to me – the blues less blue, the greens less green. When I started at the magazine, I thought it was absurd that the editors expected readers to have every colour in their mind's eye. How were they supposed to know the difference between cobalt, cerulean, aquamarine, turquoise? But I misunderstood: there was no expectation. The words were interchangeable, they just meant very blue, blue blue, sea blue. None of the writers had spent enough time in the ocean to know that there is no such thing as sea blue, that the water changes colour a thousand times a day. Last month, for a piece on the *Top Five Island Getaways (A Few Hours from New York)* I changed the words I used to describe the ocean in my copy right before we went to print. I switched *sapphire* to *azure*, *teal* to *indigo*, *blue green* to *green blue*. No one noticed.

A dendrologist from Italy told me and Arielle that the ancient Greeks thought about colour completely differently from how we do. *What do you mean?* I asked, immediately intrigued. *When Homer wrote about the sea*, she elaborated, *he never used the word* blue. The dendrologist explained the difference between *chroma*, *hue* and *value*. She took us outside and taught us how to see like the Greeks. For months after she left, we described the world to each other in terms of lightness and darkness. The sea we knew was emerald green and silvery blue, the water glittered and glistened. But that day, it was brown and black, blurred and ashen.

. . .

It must have taken only seconds from when we saw the wall of water for it to reach us, but they live as hours in my head. I replay them, over and over again. Sometimes, the memory is sharp and bright and I have perfect recall of every detail. I can step back in time and slow it down; I can look right and left, up and down, and remember exactly where everyone and everything was. I can smell the sea and feel the heat on my skin and the sand beneath my feet. But sometimes, my memories of that day are cloudy and muffled.

When I searched later for PTSD online, I found a long list of symptoms: *flashbacks, severe emotional distress, emotional numbness, memory problems, recurrent unwanted memories, upsetting nightmares, avoidance, detachment from family, fear, anxiety, hopelessness, negative thoughts about yourself.* The algorithms took note of my search. In between Facebook posts of friends on holiday around the world, ads appeared for gravity blankets and aromatherapy. I spent hours reading about the benefits of lavender and vetiver and ylang-ylang. I trawled through internet forums and saw strangers around the world quote poetry from World War I: *Always they must see these things and hear them.*

The day after that day, I heard a woman on the beach say, "It's still so beautiful." She sounded bewildered; I understood her confusion. The sky was blue again, the sun was shining brightly. She wanted the sun and the sky to express remorse on behalf of the ocean. But the Earth, callously indifferent, refused to mourn with us.

I am taken aback at just how many shades of white there are: Simply White, Cloud White, White Dove, White Heron, White Opulence, Calm, Pale Moon, Sea Wind, Desolate, Minced Onion. Who chooses to paint their house Minced Onion?

The summer Arielle and I were fourteen, we witnessed a bleaching event. Every day for three months, we watched bright corals dim before our eyes. It was like watching a Technicolor film fade to black and white. Every day, the reef turned whiter and whiter. Every day, there were fewer and fewer fish. *Bleached coral is a PR disaster*, Matthew said. *It is too beautiful.* I knew what he meant. There was no way to convince people that these gorgeous ghostly castles illuminated by the blue-green light of the ocean were a signal that the world was ending.

So many people imagine that climate change, when it comes, will be spectacular. *Spectacular*, from the Latin *spectaculum* – a spectacle, a public show, a sight. They cannot conceive of catastrophe any other way. The ocean that day was spectacular. The storm tonight might be spectacular. But most of the time devastation is quiet, subtle, humdrum.

There is a photograph of the tsunami that was shared across the world. If you cover the bottom of the image, it could be a postcard. But a third of the way down, the image transforms from pristine paradise to horror movie. I have studied it so closely that I know every pixel. Six men – three Thai hotel workers, three white foreigners – stand in the foreground. The first wave is in the background. The water is almost as high as the tops of the palm trees, which are silhouetted against a cloudless blue sky. All three of the Thai men have turned away from the water, but they do not look panicked. Only the barefoot and shirtless white man, the one closest to the water, seems to recognize the wave for what it is. His body is in motion, his calves are tensed, he looks terrified: he is attempting to flee. The man closest to the camera, dressed in light khaki pants and a dark T-shirt, is facing the approaching wave. Our perspective is aligned with his. He seems awestruck, fixed in wonder. I have never understood how this photograph was recovered. How did the Swedish tourist who took it survive? How did he keep his camera with him?

I like the names of the purples the most – Elation, Rhapsody Lilac, Vigorous Violet, Plummy, Mythical – but I return to the blues. I pick up three eight-ounce sample cans – Under the Sea (*a stately dark green that sets a dramatic mood*), Ocean Air (*a go-to blue green for creating instantly soothing spaces*) and How Blue Am I? (*blithe and easygoing, this saturated sky blue also exhibits a dash of confidence*) – and a three-inch flat brush.

"Great choices," Danny says, beaming. "I can ring you up right here." There is a little rainbow flag attached to the cash register. I notice for the first time that the flag has six colours, not seven.

We learned about the order of the colour spectrum in science class. Red, orange, yellow, green, blue, indigo, violet. I was staring out of the window looking at the neat rows of rubber trees in the plantation down the hill when our teacher said, "Roy G Biv. You can use that to help you remember the order, or," she continued, "Richard Of York Gave Battle In Vain. That's how I was taught it." Arielle looked at me, eyebrows raised. I stifled a laugh and tried to take notes. She pulled my notebook away from me and wrote out *R O Y G B I V* in the margin and started scribbling. She handed it back, a few minutes later, with her own version of the mnemonic: *Rachel Over Yonder Gives Blowjobs In Vain*. I shook my head at her, but I laughed anyway.

I put the three little cans into my bag and tuck the brush into the back pocket of my jeans.

"Stay safe out there," Danny says, as he flips the sign on the door from OPEN to CLOSED.

23.

THAILAND, Sunday, 26 December 2004

The wave overtakes me. I am plunged into darkness.

My head is pulled back, as if someone has caught hold of my hair and ripped it toward them. My ankles flip over my head. The water corkscrews my body: I spin like a top. It feels like a thousand nails are hitting me from every angle, as if I am in a washing machine full of glass. I try to take back control but it is impossible. My body twists and turns.

The next wave lifts me, dumps me, then catapults me to the surface. I gasp for air. The water surges again and returns me to the dark. I try to kick my way forward, but I am hurled sideways. Something sharp tears into my stomach. I swallow water.

I hear my father's voice telling me to relax into the current. I stop struggling and let the water have its way with me. The wave spits me to the surface.

The water drags me under again, deeper this time. Something thick and hard slams into my shoulder. A small circle of light shines below me. Arielle appears between me and the light. She beckons to me with our three-fingered wave: *Come here, trust me.* I understand: the light is above me, not below me. She disappears into the dark. I am almost out of oxygen but I kick hard and use my hands to claw toward the circle of light.

I surface. The water is moving like an oil slick, thick and black and slow. I cough: my lungs are full of liquid. The waves have taken possession of everything in their path: deck chairs, motorcycles, tables, cars, fridges, beach umbrellas. An ice-cream truck bobs in the water; a man holding on to a plank of wood emerges from behind it. He opens his mouth and then shuts it, too tired to form words. Palm trees stand firm and placid, impervious to the filthy chaos below. A woman standing on a balcony shouts something to me. I can't make out what she is saying.

A doll in a pale pink hat floats by, face down, its pale legs and arms half submerged. It's not a doll. I reach out for her, but the next wave sweeps me away.

24.

NEW YORK, Monday, 29 October 2012

The streets, usually crowded at this hour, are empty now. The birds have abandoned the trees; the wet branches rub against each other. The light has drained from the sky. A man and his dog emerge from the door of a tall apartment building. The dog, shaking slightly, lifts its leg tentatively, but nothing happens. The man pulls his coat tighter and tugs impatiently at the lead.

Three days after the tsunami, a group of dogs, their pelts wet from the ocean, started circling the bodies on the beach. I recognized them as the scavengers who hunted for scraps around the beachside restaurants. They looked ravenous. The dog at the head of the pack paused and raised its nose to the air. Two monks tried to shoo them away, but there were almost a dozen of them. We watched silently as they gorged themselves.

I cross Grand Street and see the white flag of the Soho Grand waving in the wind. The rain has made my coat heavy. When I enter, I find myself in an empty, cavernous room, but I can hear the sound of voices from above. A puddle forms at my feet. The lobby at the top of the huge staircase is loud, almost raucous. The hostess greets me warmly and offers to take my coat.

All the turquoise leather seats that line the lobby are full. People cluster around each chair. A supermodel I recognize from a billboard a few streets away is sitting on one of the armrests. She is wearing a cream turtleneck and not an ounce of makeup. She is maybe the most beautiful woman I have ever seen in real life. The rest of the room is trying not to look at her, but everyone keeps stealing glances. One of her friends bends down to whisper something in her ear, and she laughs softly. I feel jealous. There are at least five other faces I recognize – an actress and her musician boyfriend, a tennis player, a singer, a director. The mood is jovial, almost celebratory. Almost every other person has a glass of champagne in their hand.

I scan the room: Safia isn't here yet. I claim the last two

stools at the bar, in the corner. I pull out one of them and rest my soaking shoes on the gold pipe that runs a foot off the floor. The waiters are in matching uniforms: black waistcoats with five silver buttons over white dress shirts. A floral arrangement towers at the other end of the bar, the tops almost brushing the ceiling. A waiter asks me what I would like; I say I'll wait till my friend arrives. He hands me a small white towel to dry my face and hair.

Each of the four shelves behind the bar is lined with bottles of amber liquid. Scrawled across the mirror are the words AMERICAN WHISKEY. A man with slicked-back hair is talking loudly on the phone about production budgets. His companion, a grey-haired woman with high cheekbones and eyelids painted green, is looking out of the window, which is framed by heavy mustard-yellow curtains. I watch the world outside through the floor-to-ceiling mirror in front of me. Arielle, completely dry, stares longingly at the heavy rain. The waiter sets down a paper coaster and then a glass of ice water in front of me. I check my phone. There is a new email from Safia: *I'll be twenty minutes late, so sorry, work call.*

Two days after the tsunami, trucks dropped off huge blocks of dry ice and an air-conditioned tent. *The tent is for the foreigners*, the driver explained. A day later, hundreds and hundreds of coffins arrived. *Where are these coming from?* someone asked. *The prison*, a monk replied. *The prisoners are making them.* I translated for everyone around me. Another truck arrived, with smaller coffins. *An nii samrap dek dek*, the driver said, as he unloaded them. *For the children*, I translated needlessly. When we finished unloading the little wooden boxes, someone brought us bottles of Coke and we sat down on the sand to take a break. When we finished our drinks, the disaster specialists directed us to carry the coffins to the beach.

Apart from the monks and the body collectors, there were six of us who volunteered at the temple morning till night for three weeks: a fisherman, a hotel manager from farther north, a German man, a middle-aged Australian woman, a young Englishwoman and me. We were all looking for someone. The German man was looking for his younger brother; his wife kept asking him to come home. The fisherman was looking for two of his daughters. His wife was safe – she had taken their youngest child, a baby boy, to visit her parents in their village the day before the tsunami. The Englishwoman was searching for her boyfriend. The Australian woman and the hotel manager were both looking for their mothers.

We had been working wordlessly for hours one day when the Englishwoman said softly, *I hate them.* I wondered if she meant the monks or the aid workers. *Who?* I asked. *Them*, she repeated, pointing at the bodies on the beach. Her mouth was clenched, her teeth were grinding against each other. *I feel so angry at them*, she said. I was surprised that I understood exactly what she meant. *Me too*, said the Australian woman. *They found dolphins in the lagoon*, the hotel manager said, to change the subject. *The lagoon is a kilometre inland*, I explained to everyone else. *How will they get them out?* the German man asked no one in particular.

In the bar seat next to me, a man is reading a thick book with worn pages. His concentration is complete, he hasn't stopped reading since I got here. He takes out a black pen from his pocket and underlines a sentence: *for there is no folly of the beasts of the earth which is not infinitely outdone by the madness of men.* He puts the pen back in his pocket and looks up at me. I look away; he returns to the book.

I open the Notes app on my phone, and start typing quickly: *The exceptionally remote and dramatically beautiful Skeleton Coast is like nowhere else on earth.* I pause to think. *Spend the afternoon driving down the rugged beaches and across stunning dunes.* It seems deception not to mention the bones at all. *Keep an eye out for skeletons and shipwrecks.* My editor is going to hate this; he will tell me that we don't go on holiday to think about death.

UNDER WATER

. . .

The fisherman who was looking for his daughters sold mostly lobsters, crabs and stingrays to the wet markets. After we had been working side by side for a week, he told me about his last trip to sea. He had left early, well before the sun was up, just like he did every day. *The water was empty*, he said, *we didn't catch anything.* They stayed out for an hour longer than usual and still nothing. Then, just as they were about to head back, the surface of the water erupted. Thousands of fish were jumping on the surface. *It looked like they were dancing*, he said. He and his partner used their nets to scoop them up. They didn't normally catch fish, but this was too easy. *We felt so lucky*, he said, *but I should have known.* He fell silent. *What did he say?* the Australian woman asked me. I tried to describe the fish the way he had, but I couldn't find the right words in English. I told her that the man said he should have known the tsunami was coming. She reached over and touched the fisherman's hand. *We couldn't have known*, she said. The fisherman shook his head and looked down at his feet, refusing the consolation.

The wind starts lashing against the windows. The man closes his book. (The whale on the cover isn't the same species as the one in the story.) Both of us turn to watch. The billboard outside – a Calvin Klein underwear ad – sways violently. The man's shirt has a tiny Red Cross logo on the sleeve. I realize that he is here for the storm. His phone rings, and he answers. He talks quietly and urgently into it for a few minutes: "It's not looking good . . . I don't know . . . I'll head out first thing . . . I can't do anything right now . . ." While he's speaking he gestures for the bill. He scrawls down his room number, signs and then leaves. He forgets to take the novel. I slip it off the counter into my bag.

After the tsunami, the Thai government sent workers to collect DNA samples from the most unrecognizable bodies. The workers arrived clad in gas masks and white protective suits, with canisters of disinfectant hanging across their backs. They assigned each nameless corpse a unique code. Then the dentists arrived, each trailed by a photographer. The dentists conducted examinations to make records that might be used to identify the dead, and the photographers took a picture of each body. When they were done, we covered the corpses with black tarps, and the body collectors took them away to mass graves.

For weeks after the tsunami, Arielle's parents donated twenty of the rooms at the hotel to international aid workers. I refused to go back to the island for weeks so that I could spend all my nights in our room. I thought maybe Arielle would walk back through the lobby doors. I sat at breakfast and watched the aid workers tuck into the buffet. They had come from across the world only to focus their efforts in Phuket, even though other parts of the country were as devastated. (The hotels in Phuket were nicer.) Years later, I saw one of them on a news show talking about differing rates of mortality by age and gender in natural disasters. *In Sri Lanka in 2004, children died disproportionately because they were less capable of swimming than adults,* she told the host, *but in Japan in 2011, the opposite was true.* Of the nearly quarter of a million people who died in the tsunami, estimates suggest that between a third and a half were children.

I see Safia before she sees me. She is wearing a cream silk shirt and black trousers; her hair falls in loose curls over her shoulders. She looks like an adult. Most people found Safia and Zara uncanny. Everything about them seemed to match – the way their faces moved, the way they flicked their wrists when they were irritated, the way they ran, the way they laughed. But if you knew them, it was easy to tell the difference: Safia's nose was slightly straighter, Zara's eyes were a shade lighter, Safia had more freckles on her right cheek, Zara had a wider forehead.

We embrace tightly, then we sit down and start catching

each other up on the last two years of our lives. She won the big case she was working on the last time I saw her, her parents just moved back to Berlin, she's started playing football again, quite seriously. I tell her that my father is doing well, that I'm not running the marathon this year, and that I know I should look for another job but I haven't started yet. The waiter finally returns to take our order: I ask for a Manhattan, Safia orders a Rob Roy and fries. When the waiter leaves, she opens her mouth to say something but then takes a sip of water instead.

I ask her how she really is.

"I look in the mirror and try to see her. I try to make my eyes her eyes, my cheekbones her cheekbones, my freckles her freckles. Most of the time it doesn't work, but sometimes it does and I can see her again. My colleagues think I'm a narcissist because I look at every mirror I pass."

I want to tell her that she has unwittingly recounted a version of the Narcissus myth — not the familiar one where he is obsessed with his own reflection, but the one where he is mourning the twin sister who looked just like him — but I don't want to interrupt her. She dips a fry in ketchup, then puts it back down on the plate without taking a bite.

"I don't know if you remember, but when we were in grade eight, Zara fell off a bike on the way home and broke her leg.

You, me and Arielle were playing a match at school and I suddenly felt a sharp pain in my leg. I was about to be subbed in and I told Coach M that I couldn't play, my leg hurt. He thought I was making an excuse because I was too nervous. But I was in so much pain. When I got home in the evening, I found out about Zara. I never told anyone about it. Not even her. It was too weird. I thought everyone would think I was making it up."

She stops and stares into her plate. She asks the bartender for chilli sauce – "the hottest you have" – and I wait for her to continue. "I haven't told anyone in London that I'm a twin. No one in my life now knows that there were two of us." Safia scratches the small scar above her eyebrow and takes another sip of her drink. "Sometimes I catch myself thinking in *we*s. We like this. We hate that. And then I remember there is no *we*. I am an *I* now."

I can't remember much about our last term at school. We went back to classrooms full of empty chairs. We were left silent by shock. I sat in my old seat next to the chair that Arielle used to sit in. There were new divisions among us during those last few months at school: those who had been there and those who had been away; those who had lost family and those who had not. Alliances shifted. Those of us who had been caught in the water could only stand to be around one another. Those who hadn't lost best friends resented those who had, for being proprietary with our grief. They wanted to share it with us — they were their friends too — but we didn't want to let them in.

"How are *you*?" Safia asks.

"I miss her every day." The words almost catch in my throat. I am about to continue when the room is pitched into darkness. It is silent at first, and then the room starts to fill with shouts and nervous laughter.

A voice cuts through the dark: "Please stay where you are. We will bring candles to all the tables." In a few minutes, the lobby and bar are lit by a dozen flames moving through the air. The voice speaks again: "Drinks are on us tonight, folks." Cheers all around. A piano starts playing and a voice begins to sing a familiar song. Everyone stops talking to listen. When the duo finish, the room applauds and conversation resumes. Less than twenty minutes have passed when the lights buzz, flicker and come back on. Cheers again.

"I should get going," I say.

"How are you going to get home?" Safia asks. I lie and say I live less than two blocks away.

"You can stay here, you know."

"It's really close."

"You really can stay. The bed is huge." She sounds worried. "I don't think you should go outside."

"It'll take me three minutes."

"Okay." She knows I'm lying. "This was so nice. I've missed you. Let's not leave it so long next time. Text me when you get home."

"I will," I say. We hug a long goodbye. Downstairs, the doorman tries to stop me leaving – "It's not safe out there!" – but I ignore him and walk back outside.

25.

THAILAND, Sunday, 26 December 2004

I come back to consciousness on a mattress next to half a boat. I recognize the 7-Eleven on the street corner: I am miles inland. The streets are littered with debris: furniture, suitcases, glass, toys, televisions, cushions, broken mirrors. A red sofa is resting on top of a car; a thick tree trunk lies across the road; a speedboat is on the pavement. A Thai flag, stripped from its mast, is on the ground. There are piles and piles of wood everywhere. The back half of a bus is sticking out of a shop. There is a shadow in the tree above me: a body. One arm sticks out at an impossible angle, the head droops to one side, the feet are bare.

People are staggering through the road, shouting names. A

woman with nothing on below the waist is roving madly. The lacerations on her back are exposed through rips in her T-shirt. Her eyes scan the splintered wood that covers the streets as she calls, "Dao, Dao, Dao, Dao, Dao." She stops, something has made her silent. She bends down, picks up a little shoe and starts screaming.

A heavily pregnant woman is wading through the shallow water. Her full belly is pressed against her white linen shirt and the darkness of her belly button is visible. She stares blankly at the ground. "I can't feel him," she says. She digs her feet into the ground, as if she is trying to push the earth away. "I can't feel him," she says again, to no one.

A mewling fills the air. A baby rests atop a pile of broken wood. Another woman runs to it. I can tell from the way she looks at it that it is not hers, but she picks the baby up tenderly. The crying gets louder. The woman cradles the baby in her arms and starts shushing it.

I feel a tap on my shoulder. It is a man wearing no shirt. "Khun okay mai?" he asks. I try to respond but no sound comes out. "Okay?" he says again. He has a deep gash on his thigh, just below his right hip, and blood drips thickly down his leg. I point at his wound and he nods. He points at my stomach. I look down and see it is sliced open. He walks away. *Why did he leave me?* I think, *please come back*. He does, with a long deep blue cloth. He's torn a piece from the flag. He bends down next to me and presses the cloth into my stomach to stop the bleeding. I bite my arm hard to stop myself from screaming. The world grows quiet around me, colour drains away, my peripheral vision blurs then fades. "I can't hear," I tell him, "I can't see." He leaves again. He returns with a can of 7UP. "Here," he says. "Drink." He opens the can and holds it to my mouth. Within minutes, colour floods back, volume returns. I hear a voice shouting for help. A man is trapped under a fallen tree.

"Khun chuay khao dai mai," I tell the shirtless man. He is surprised at my Thai, but he nods and goes to help the trapped man. He shouts for a knife. Somehow, another man produces one. The two men take turns to cut away the trunk using a small kitchen knife. The man stuck underneath screams and screams. After ten minutes, they pull him free and he passes out.

I use a broken table to pull myself up to stand. There is a boy lying on the ground with a two-inch hole in the middle of his chest, a sucking wound. His lips are a deep blue. A man I recognize as one of the local dive instructors digs into his wet bag and pulls out a tube. It's silicone paste, the same brand Matthew uses to seal his camera before a dive. The instructor smears the paste onto a piece of cloth and presses it to the boy's chest. In seconds, his chest rises again.

UNDER WATER

. . .

The shirtless man comes back with a teenage boy and a motorcycle. They help me to get on the back of the bike; I wrap my arms around the teenager's waist.

"He will take you to the hospital," the man tells me in Thai.

"Khop khun maak na kha," I say, knowing that words are not enough. "Thank you very much."

"Mai tong khob khun rok." He presses my hands between his. "No need."

Most of the roads to the hospital have buckled and cracked, as if they have been ripped apart hastily by invisible hands. I hold on tight. Each bump is agonizing; I press my lips together to keep from crying out. The boy has to swerve to avoid a naked man and woman who stumble out in front of us. The wave has stripped them of everything. They look like Adam and Eve thrown out of Eden.

26.

NEW YORK, Monday, 29 October 2012

The wind is fierce, freezing and slightly salty. The rain is coming down in heavy sheets and the roads have already started to flood. In seconds, I am soaked to the bone. *Finally*, I think. The streets are dark and deserted. None of the other buildings have their power back. There is no electricity anywhere: the streetlights are off, the traffic lights are dark. I can barely see a few feet ahead of me. I have to lean forward into the wind in order to walk without falling over.

The sound of sirens grows louder. Arielle steps out from behind a parked car. She walks to me easily, undisturbed by the elements. *Marissa, she says, what are you doing?* I keep struggling against the wind. A police car pulls up. The officer rolls down the window and shouts over the wind. I can't hear him. He shouts louder. "You need to get inside." I ignore him. I take a step forward and the wind pushes me into a wall. "Get inside now, ma'am." I stare at him defiantly. "Now!"

He's right, Arielle says. *This is dangerous. And stupid.*

"Leave me alone." The officer thinks I am talking to him. Anger flashes in his eyes, but he gets a call on the radio and drives away. Arielle vanishes into the air.

The storm is rampaging through the streets. A motorbike is lying flat in the middle of the pavement, broken branches are flying through the air, a metal trash can rolls noisily down the road. The wind is battering the trees. The noise is thunderous.

I turn right onto Canal Street and a gust nearly takes me off my feet. Water is surging through the streets. The rising river is heading straight toward me. I fight to take another step forward. Arielle appears, across the road. She beckons to me with our three-fingered wave – *Come here, trust me* – and I go, as if pulled by a string. I push my way through the wind, using my hands to protect my face from flying branches. Something cuts through my palm.

When I get there, she is gone. The same police car is parked exactly where she was standing. The officer doesn't bother to reason with me this time. He gets out of the car and the wind strips him of his hat. He opens the back door and pushes me inside. He climbs back in, enraged, and asks me where I live. I give him my address. "What the fuck are you doing down here?"

I don't say a word the whole way home.

27.

THAILAND, Sunday, 26 December 2004

The motorcycle stops, and the teenage boy helps me walk to the main entrance of the hospital. Two nurses are guarding the doors, deciding who is hurt badly enough to be let in. I join the end of the line – there are about thirty people in front of me – and sit on the ground, leaning against a wall to rest.

Every Thai person who is able is doing something to help: a skinny man is handing out pieces of fruit, a woman is carrying a big bottle of water and pouring it into people's mouths, a couple is offering their phones to anyone who needs to make a call. Most of the foreigners are still in a state of mute confusion.

A young woman on the ground stretches her hand out to

accept a phone. She takes a few seconds to remember the number before she dials. "It's me," she says in an American accent. "I'm okay. Tell my dad I'm okay. I don't know where I am, but I'm okay."

A few steps away from the main entrance to the hospital, a makeshift medical station has formed. A man is standing barefoot on the hood of a car and handing out orders – *cut this cloth, bring more water, find scissors.* He orders two boys to go look for first aid boxes at nearby restaurants. They set off running down the street. Next to the shoeless man, a man with his arms covered in black mud is translating into Dublin-accented English for the tourists.

A bearded man approaches the Irishman.

"I am a doctor," he says. "I worked in the war. In Bosnia. I can help."

The Irishman nods, pauses to think, and then raises his voice again. "If you have any medical training, please come here."

A small group of tourists gathers in front of him – two women who identify themselves as nurses from Italy, a broad-shouldered Australian man trained as an EMT, a middle-aged Indian doctor and a slender Frenchwoman who is a surgeon. The Bosnian doctor speaks to them with quiet authority for a few minutes. They listen attentively, then get to work.

The two boys return with a collection of first aid boxes and present them to the Bosnian doctor. He opens them and pulls out tiny vials of iodine and Mercurochrome. Another boy arrives with a huge bottle of painkillers; the Italian nurses start dispensing tablets to the crowd. A girl of about sixteen, her hair in pigtails, approaches the Irishman and says, "I can help too. Please." He tells her to ask the nurses for some bandages, and then tells her the word for bandage in Thai.

A man arrives at the entrance to the hospital pushing a supermarket trolley with a limp girl inside. We let him go to the front of the line. A nurse checks for a pulse and shakes her head. The man starts to whimper.

When I get to the front of the line, the nurse looks at my stomach and immediately ushers me through the doors. Inside, it is chaos. People are screaming, shouting, crying, gasping, vomiting, bleeding. Children are catatonic, adults are hysterical. I sit down on the edge of a hospital bed. A man carries in a woman draped over his shoulders; she is missing half a leg and the white of her femur is sticking out. A young man arrives with a large chunk of wood stuck in his shoulder. Another man is missing half the skin on his forehead. Uniformed nurses are trying to clean wounds, but they have run out of saline. Someone brings a bucket of water.

On the bed next to mine, a blonde woman is shaking and

sweating. She keeps raising her head to ask for help but her words are slurred. I ask her if she is okay. "I'm diabetic," she says slowly. I stop a nurse rushing past us. I don't know the word for diabetes but I tell the nurse in Thai, "Her sugar is low." The nurse shakes me off and disappears. "I'm sorry," I say to the blonde woman. "I tried to tell her." I don't know if I've used the right word for sugar, maybe there is a different word for blood sugar. But the nurse is back with a box of mango juice. I put the straw in the box and hand it to the lady.

I hear a voice I recognize and look up to see Safia moving madly from bed to bed. I know immediately that she is looking for Zara. Her clothes are soaking and the skin above her eyebrow is split. Blood is caked on her cheek. A young doctor wearing thin-rimmed glasses gestures for me to sit on an empty bed.

"You need stitches," he says, pointing at my stomach.

"I have to go to my friend," I reply, pointing at Safia.

"I need to stitch you first," he insists, and he touches my shoulder with such tenderness that I start to cry. I lie down on the bed and he sews me together. I gasp each time the needle pierces my skin.

A nurse, running from bed to bed checking patients, is trying to maintain order amid the madness. But when she sees Safia, she freezes, wild-eyed with fear. She looks toward the bed in the corner of the room where a sheet is covering a body, then back at Safia. Safia stops, and then slowly walks over to the sheet and pulls it back. She crumples to the floor. A keening fills the room.

Where are you? I think. *Where are you?*

28.

NEW YORK, Monday, 29 October 2012

I strip out of my soaking clothes and step into the shower. The water is so hot my skin stings, but I stay under until I stop shivering. When I get out, I dry myself, put lotion on my scars, and get into a thick sweater and a pair of sweatpants. I turn on a nature documentary and unload my bag onto the counter: three little cans of paint, two mini skull candles, a box of matches from the restaurant yesterday, the loaf of bread, the can of condensed milk and both novels. The storm continues to rage outside. I make myself a cup of tea; I'm still cold.

On the screen, a pack of dholes is moving through a thick forest. A deep male voice is speaking. "The dholes are hunting a wild boar and her piglets." The camera cuts to the boar: she stops chewing and raises her head. She is on high alert. "The new mother can sense danger." Three piglets emerge from behind the trees. The dholes' auburn coats vanish into the grass. "The dholes must work together. They need to get their timing exactly right." Six dholes pounce in tandem; they devour the mother while her children watch.

For Arielle's seventh birthday, her grandparents gave her a subscription to Oxford Scientific Films. Every month, she received twelve new cards that she'd organize into groups in the black-and-blue binder. Each card was full of facts – habitat, population, behaviour, characteristics – about a different animal from around the world. Dholes, I remember, live in the forests of South and Southeast Asia. They remodel hyena dens to use as their own, and they are social creatures who live in packs, or sometimes in couples.

I keep Arielle's binder on the kitchen table, next to the pair of binoculars I inherited from my mother. For the past few years, when an animal goes extinct, I remove their file from the binder and place it in a separate folder.

Arielle is singing softly, a familiar song whose title I can't recall, and leafing through the extinction pile.

How did you get this?

"Your mother gave it to me before I left for college. She wanted me to have it."

The documentary has moved on to tigers. I tear two slices of white bread into small pieces and dip them straight into the open can of condensed milk. I have forgotten how sweet it is; my teeth start to ache. As a pair of tiger cubs roll in the mud, the narrator explains, "The tiger population in the jungles of Karnataka in India is exploding." A local park ranger is speaking proudly about the success of the programme as he drives a safari vehicle down a dusty road. I recognize that accent. I look closely at the logo on the vehicle: this is the same jungle where Matthew learned how to take photos of wild animals. Arielle sits down next to me on the sofa. *Unless they are magically expanding the forest*, she says, *more tigers means less of something else*. I leave the sofa and start lining the floor with yesterday's newspaper.

Rosie, my father, Nik and Katerina were on a dive when the tsunami hit. The visibility was terrible, the currents were difficult. Despite all their experience, they had trouble staying together underwater. *There were no fish,* my father told me weeks later. *It was as if they had evacuated.* Rosie knew immediately something wasn't right, but she didn't know what. When they got back to the boat, Anurak refused to take them to the island. Instead, he took them farther out to sea. *We are safer here*, he told them. Matthew had decided at the last minute to stay at the cottage to finish a piece. When Rosie and my father got back to the island hours later, he was missing.

The cottage and the lab were completely destroyed. Hard drives with three years of data, samples from the whole year, full notebooks, all gone. The guesthouse was still standing, protected by a row of trees. The only thing on the island that remained untouched was the tree house. The surrounding reefs were scoured clean. For weeks after, fragments of coral and detached mangrove roots hung suspended in the waters around the beach. Matthew's body washed ashore three days later.

My father and Anurak took the boat to the mainland to come search for us as soon as they could. My father found me in the hospital, and he took me back to the hotel. Arielle's parents gave us adjoining rooms. He went back to the island in the mornings to start rebuilding, but he spent every night with me. After a week, he pleaded with me to come back home. I refused. *Nik and Katerina have gone home*, he tried again, *it's just me and Rosie*. I wouldn't go: I needed to keep looking.

Grief pushed us in opposite directions. My father didn't want to leave – *Thailand is my home*, he said, without a hint of irony. I couldn't wait to get away. I hated the new ghost town. The beaches were devoid of tourists for months. Restaurants and bars reopened, months later, for nobody. Loud music played to empty rooms, plastic chairs vibrated along the floor, waiters stood by vacant tables, bartenders cleaned unused glasses. All of us who grew up wishing the tourists would stay away wanted them to come back.

There is a loud bang outside. I remove the chilli plant from the sill and place it on the floor so I can press my face against the window. The rain is punishing the canopy in the park; the trees are careening wildly. I can't see the street below. I go back to the kitchen and pour myself a glass of wine. I scroll through my phone looking for news about the storm. The power plant on East Thirteenth Street exploded at 9 p.m. Someone has already uploaded a video of the explosion: it is one minute and twenty-six seconds long. I watch it five times in a row. The top comment reads: *This knocked out the entire grid in lower Manhattan.* The first reply is: *I live on 12th and 5th, no power here.* The second reply is: *I'm on 22nd Street and I have power.* In almost every reply that follows, people state their location and whether they do or do not have power.

I use a butter knife to pry open the sample can of Ocean Air. Arielle is lying on the floor, a few feet away, drawing squares in the dust with her finger. I find a spot on the floor near the window and start painting the wall with thin, light strokes. Arielle tells me she doesn't like the colour. She's starting to annoy me. I continue to make my way across the wall. There is a particular pleasure in covering the first light coat with a second and a third so that the cracks fade then disappear completely.

The documentary has moved, without explanation, from South India to East Africa. A leopard is lazing on a tree branch. *In Tanzania, the Zanzibar leopard, a subspecies of the mainland leopard, was hunted because many people believed they were used by witches.* The voiceover starts listing other species that have been declared extinct over the past thirty years. *Earlier this year, the last Pinta Island tortoise died. His name was Lonesome George.* The documentary shows the last photograph ever taken of the endling: saggy flesh, droopy eyes, waiting for the end.

Poor George, Arielle says, staring at the screen. Anger twitches in my chest. I keep painting, focusing on going in straight lines, trying to make a perfect square. Paint drips onto my forearm.

Hey, I hear her say, *I'm sorry.*

I feel my eyes glaze over. For a minute, I don't speak. I don't move. Anger turns my face hot and makes my fingers tingle. How dare she. How dare she run toward the water, how dare she leave me alone. I turn to face her. "Why didn't you run with me?" She doesn't answer. I take off my sweater. My fury makes me hot.

"I could swim my way out of it, why couldn't you? We were creatures of the sea, remember?" I see her elbow jerk slightly, but she still refuses to answer.

"Answer me," I scream. "Why didn't you run?"

I watch a different version of myself pick up the half-drunk glass of wine and launch it against the newly painted wall. Shards of glass rain across the newspaper on the floor. Arielle looks at me, then walks through the wall without saying a word.

I bend down slowly to pick up the broken pieces. Some of the glass is now flecked with Ocean Air. I step on a shard and wince. I pluck it out of the sole of my foot, and blood drips onto the newspaper.

I wrap my foot in a towel and sit down on my bed. It wasn't Arielle's fault. It was mine. I told a boyfriend once that I was to blame. He said, *Do you know how many people died that day?* He thought I was being ludicrous. I knew as soon as he said it that our relationship was over. He didn't understand. No one understood.

Arielle didn't want to go back to the hotel on Christmas. She wanted to stay on the island, she wanted to go diving with my father and Rosie on Boxing Day. She wanted to be there when the pregnant mantas were tagged. I insisted, she resisted.

I sulked, she relented. She didn't want to fight. I lie down and start to sob. "I'm sorry," I keep saying. "I'm sorry."

When I wake up, sun is streaming through the window and Arielle is sitting at the foot of my bed, *Come home,* she says to me. *It's been too long.*

Home

"But they are dead; those two are dead!
Their spirits are in heaven!"
'Twas throwing words away; for still
The little Maid would have her will,
And said, "Nay, we are seven!"

William Wordsworth

I never saw a wild thing
sorry for itself.

DH Lawrence

I am in a candy store. The lights are fluorescent and the walls are painted in thick neon swirls. Clear glass jars filled with candy of different shapes, sizes and colours line the walls. Coca-Cola bottles, red Ferraris, raspberry drops, vanilla marshmallows, jelly snakes, green apple straws, rainbow dummies.

A young clerk, blonde and bright-eyed, bounces up to me. She is wearing a red-and-white polka-dot dress. She takes me by the hand and pulls me toward some jars. She pops off a lid, reaches in with a pair of metal tongs, and places a translucent red candy shaped like a flattened strawberry in the palm of my hand. It's delicious. Before I've finished chewing, she has pulled out three more: a lime-green frog, a black licorice car, a sugary lemon skull. *Try them*, she implores. *These are my favourites*. The lemon skull fizzes in my mouth and disappears in seconds. I bite off the frog's head, and it is so sour that my mouth fills with water. The licorice is bitter; I chase it with the rest of the frog.

Come with me, she says, gesturing to the corner of the room where a curtain covers an open doorway. We walk through the curtain and step into a dark, carpeted room. There are more glass jars, but they are bigger, heavier. The signs above them advertise various ailments: DEPRESSION, DIGESTION, HEART HEALTH, THYROID, JOINT CARE. The girl moves toward the jar labelled HEADACHE and plucks out something round and red. She scoops out some powder from RHEUMATISM, divides it into two mugs, and pours hot water from a thermos to make tea. She inhales the rising steam and smiles. She hands me a mug and lifts her hand, encouraging me to drink. I sip it slowly. It tastes like cinnamon, honey and something else. I notice the corner of a photograph sticking out from under the RHEUMATISM jar. I pull it out. It is a young boy with light brown skin wearing crutches. One leg is amputated above the knee. He is smiling, a big toothless smile. I pick up the wooden scoop for the rheumatism powder to read the label tied to it with a red-and-white string: *tibia and teeth.*

29.

THAILAND, Wednesday, 26 December 2012

I put one foot into the boat and it sways beneath me. I reach for a wooden plank to steady myself and a splinter slips into the palm of my hand. I wince. I hold out my hand to Anurak as if I were a child. He holds my wrist steady with one hand and plucks out the splinter with the other thumb and forefinger. He flicks the tiny piece of wood into the water and then presses down on my palm to soothe the pain.

"Khop khun kha," I say. My voice trembles.

"Man jep mai?" he asks, concerned. I shake my head, it doesn't hurt.

"Yin dii thii khun klap maa baan khrap," he says.

"Chan duay," I reply. I'm glad I'm home too.

His eyes fill and he starts the motor. Once we are moving, I put my hand out to touch the surface of the sea and let the water slip through my open fingers. *It is so blue*, I think. The sun caresses my skin, the sea sprays across my face, and my body relaxes.

I turn to face the front of the boat so I can watch as the island comes into view. My father and Anurak rebuilt each building – the cottage, the lab, the guesthouse – one at a time, over the course of a year. *Matthew would have been much better at all of this than any of us*, I remember my father saying when they were halfway through. *His tree house is still standing strong.*

Anurak rounds the corner and the island appears. From here, the three buildings look exactly as they did before. My father and Rosie are standing on the beach, ankles in the water, waiting. They wave; I stand and wave back. Before Anurak can fully stop the boat, I jump into the water. I run to hug my father first, and then Rosie.

"Are you hungry?" Rosie asks me. I nod silently. If I speak, I will cry. My father stays silent too. "Good. Your father has been cooking for you all morning."

I open the door and my mouth instantly waters from the smell of garlic and chilli frying in hot oil. I follow my father back to the stove; he's made all my favourites: miang kham, haw mok and crab curry. Fresh dough for pa thong ko is sitting on the counter.

"Who made this?" I ask, pointing at the dough.

"Arielle's mother sent it from the hotel. Aroon made it especially for you."

"Who else is here?" I ask.

"No one," says Rosie. "It's just us. No guests until the new year."

"Do you need any help with anything?"

"No," she says. "Why don't you go outside for a bit?"

"Do you want to take your bag to your room before you go?" my father asks. He sounds almost shy. I realize he's nervous.

"Yes," I reply, and I realize I'm nervous too. I pull my suitcase into the room and close the door. The bed is perfectly made. My father has bought toiletries and set up a little dresser. He's even tried to recreate the small collection of books that Arielle and I kept here: *The Mill on the Floss*, *Tess of the d'Urbervilles*, *Emma*, *Orlando*, *The Bluest Eye*. Exam books mixed with some of our own. A lump forms in my throat. There is a photograph of the two of us, laughing on the boat after a dive, framed on the bedside table. Next to it is a photo from when I was six. I'm sitting on Matthew's shoulders, reaching for a flower on a branch.

. . .

Both the kayaks are already parked on the sand; my father knows where I want to go. I drag the red kayak, her kayak, and head to our beach. The sky is light blue, the water is calm and clear. Soon, my skin starts to prickle under the bright sun. A hawksbill joins me, swimming serenely by my side all the way there.

The beach is covered with tiny balls of sand arranged in radial patterns; the bubbler crabs have been feasting since low tide. I crush hundreds of balls under my feet as I make my way to the rocks to look out at the open ocean. Light trips across the surface of the water. A cloud drifts across the sun, and the emerald water darkens and then brightens again. I jump in, feet first.

The reef is humming with life: black-and-white angelfish, multicolour parrotfish, sunshine-yellow boxfish with black polka dots, flat batfish, long-nosed butterfly fish, fat-lipped triggerfish, freckled goatfish, spiky lionfish. A battery of barracuda patrols the shallows. I kick my way through them and they disperse and then gather again. A pufferfish floats past sedately. A blue-spotted stingray swims just above the sea floor. The sand below it shakes, and the black eyes of a maimed flounder survey the world above. Two surgeonfish pluck algae from the coral.

From the deep, three manta rays soar into the reef. They head straight to me: Lizzie, Lily and Anna K. I turn my body horizontal, my face to the surface of the water. The mantas come so close that I can look into their eyes. They take turns swimming in circles around me.

I stay with them for as long as I can hold my breath.

Acknowledgments

I remember exactly where I was when I received my first email from Sebastian Godwin. It ended, "If you already have a literary agent, lucky them." I did not, lucky me. For his endless patience, constant encouragement, sensitivity and inconceivable willingness to laugh at my jokes, I am eternally grateful. Thanks also to the rest of the team at DGA: Aparna Kumar, Heather Godwin and especially David Godwin, whose early faith in me and my writing meant the world.

I am deeply indebted to Becky Saletan for the care and attention she has shown to both me and this book. From our first meeting, I knew I was in the safest of hands. She saw what needed to be done and made it easy for me to do it. Thanks also to the rest of the team at Riverhead: Delia Taylor, Glory Ann Plata, Ashley Garland, Nora Alice Demick, Lauren Peters-Collaer, Alexis Sulaimani, Nicole Celli, Jynne Dilling Martin and Geoff Kloske.

Ravi Mirchandani was the first stranger to tell me he liked the book. It still feels surreal to me. Thank you for shepherding it into the world. Working with the team at Summit and Simon & Schuster UK has been an absolute pleasure from day one. Amy Fletcher and Ben Phillips, the world's best rights team, made September and

ACKNOWLEDGMENTS

October 2024 the best kind of roller coaster. Suzanne Baboneau took the reins at a crucial time and showed me what it was to lead with grace. Thanks also to: Reuben Bharucha, Polly Osborn, Olivia Allen, Joe Christie, Genevieve Barratt and Ami Smithson. Finally, Rebecca Servadio of London Literary Scouting – whatever you did, it made a huge difference. Thank you.

My research for this book was deep and varied – meteorological reports, academic research papers, IPCC reports, research trips to Thailand, firsthand accounts from tsunami survivors, newspaper articles about both the 2004 tsunami and Hurricane Sandy, narrative nonfiction about invasive species and biomass loss, documentaries about rainforests and coral reefs. I cannot hope to name all my sources, but a few were essential: *Manta: Secret Life of Devil Rays* by Guy Stevens and Thomas Peschak; *Guide to the Manta & Devil Rays of the World* by Guy Stevens, Daniel Fernando, Marc Dando and Giuseppe Notarbartolo di Sciara; *Thailand: Traveller's Wildlife Guide* by David L Pearson and Les Beletsky; *Birds of Thailand* by Craig Robson; *Reef Life* by Brandon Cole; *Ghosts of the Tsunami* by Richard Lloyd Parry; *Wave* by Sonali Deraniyagala; *Wave of Destruction* by Erich Krauss; "The Sea was Never Blue" by Maria Michela Sassi; and Rob Perryman's academic papers on manta rays, especially "Social preferences and network structure in a population of reef manta rays." I also relied on the many resources made available to the members of Manta Trust. A huge thank you to Andrea Marshall, Queen of Mantas, for replying to an email from a total stranger, speaking to me for over an hour on Zoom, and answering my many random questions about the day-to-day realities of researching manta rays. I hope you'll forgive any inaccuracies. For help with the Thai: Shrutika Sachdev and Ratana Sachdev. For making sure

ACKNOWLEDGMENTS

every Thai sentence was perfect and standardized: David Atherton. I owe you one.

At various stages, I have turned to many people for support, counsel, encouragement and help of various kinds: Daniel Blank, Nicola Chang, Sarah Dimick, Naomi Levine, Raven Leilani, Jesse McCarthy, David Means, Sonya Posmentier, Adam Ross, Jess Row and Michelle Sterling. Danya Weiss told me that it seemed that all I really wanted to do was to write a novel, and that I should probably do that. I don't think I would have stayed the course if not for her clarity.

I was able to write this book because my brilliant professors at Columbia University taught me how to read: Nicholas Dames, Jenny Davidson, Alan Stewart, James Shapiro, Julie Crawford, Molly Murray, Flora Armetta and Erik Gray. Erik, I've never stopped thinking about *In Memoriam*. I hope you don't mind that I stole one of your lines. I spent my seven years at NYU reading nineteenth-century novels, walking the streets of New York and idling in bookstores. For teaching me how to read better, think better, write better: Catherine Robson and Maureen McLane. For handselling the best novels I've read over the last decade: the booksellers of Three Lives & Company, especially Troy. Graduate school sometimes made it easy to forget why I had decided to spend my life in books; whenever I walked through those red doors, I remembered. Getting to spend three glorious years at the Harvard Society of Fellows has been one of my greatest fortunes. For the gift of time, the Senior Fellows. For making everything run smoothly, and for her friendship, Ana Novak. For every conversation, every debate, every laugh, every glass: the JFs and their other halves.

I am indebted to friends and family who read drafts and gave comments at every stage. The early readers: Gabriel Mohr, Pedro

ACKNOWLEDGMENTS

Regalado, Heba Gowayed and Katrin Dias. For keeping pace during the final push: Nora Diamond-Jones, Lauren Moran, Gili Kliger, Karuna Menon, Harmon Siegel, Ash Anderson, Shona Findlay, Anna Seigal. Nora, thank you also for your unconditional support at every stage. For reading full drafts: Emma Adler, John Clegg, Teju Cole, Jon Franklin, Shobha Karunakaran, Govind Karunakaran, Laura Mucha, Eoghan Quinn, Namwali Serpell, Louisa Thomas, Adaner Usmani and Shabana Usmani. Namwali, thank you for each of your (many) meticulous edits, and all your counsel. Teju, thank you for attending to the rhythm of every sentence. Laura, thank you for your tireless (and immeasurable) work over the last few years.

Arielle and Marissa are entirely made up, but my life has been made rich by relationships like theirs. Too many to name, but special mention: Sitara Menon, Rhea Menon, Natalie DeBoursac, Amy Sutton, Katrin Dias, Harriet Kyaw Thaung, Shona Findlay, Mallika Sachdeva, Yoshiko Shimada, Sian Williams, Erin Muldoon, Rosario Quiroz, Nora Diamond, Leeza Mangaldas, Irene Alvarado, Katherine Fitzgerald, Molly Luft, MC Hyland, Laura Yoder, Melissa Apperson and Inés Escobar González.

Rahul Menon, best of brothers, thank you for reading drafts, answering questions, giving advice, finding illustrations. All I could do was write a book about the natural world; I'm in awe that you have dedicated your life to trying to save it. Without my parents, Shobha and Govind Karunakaran, none of this would be possible. I read because they do. Thank you for keeping a house full of books and always telling me to do what makes me happy. Last and most, Adaner Usmani: even superlatives don't do justice. At least once a day I think how lucky I am to spend this life with you. Thank you for everything.